BROKEN SKIES

BROKEN SKIES

A NEW DAWN™ BOOK 5

AMY HOPKINS

MICHAEL ANDERLE

DISRUPTIVE IMAGINATION

DEDICATION

To all the parents who've ever had to work at home during the school holidays.
I salute you. You are warriors, and saints.

— Amy

To Family, Friends and
Those Who Love
to Read.
May We All Enjoy Grace
to Live The Life We Are
Called.

—Michael

CHAPTER ONE

Julianne and Marcus walked down the familiar path leading into Tahn. They'd dismounted some time ago, letting the horses rest after a frantic trip through the Madlands.

"I could have taken him," Julianne said.

Marcus blinked, as thoughts dragged back to their earlier conversation after a period of weary silence. "I told you, that remnant was too big. He'd have squashed you."

"You're not actually any taller than me," Julianne noted. "Well… maybe a finger-width, but not enough to make a difference."

"It's not about height." Marcus patted his rifle, now securely strapped to his saddlebags, and straightened his shoulders. "It's about strength, dexterity, precision in the face of—" His words stopped short as he stumbled on a rock, hidden by the lengthening shadows and washed out colors of dusk.

"You were saying?" Julianne asked with a laugh. "Tell me again how precise you are."

"Shut up." Marcus focused his eyes ahead, trying to will the heat from his cheeks. "You know what I meant."

"You meant that you were too scared to take the beast on in a fair fight, so you assumed I would be, too." Julianne lifted her hand and rubbed her thumb across a jagged bit of nail on one of her fingers. She'd broken it in the fight earlier. "You know what they say about people who assume things?"

"That Marcus is an ass," he grumped. "Fine. Maybe you could have taken him. But why? This rifle isn't for decoration. If we'd waited for you to fight off old fish-breath, we wouldn't have made it out of the Mads until well after dark. And blow a fair fight—I'm dying for a soft bed, Jules."

"Well, it's all behind us now," Julianne consoled him. "We're past the big mean remnants keeping you from your beauty sleep. We can—"

A hiss cut her off, and her horse skittered to one side as a figure leaped out from behind a tree.

"Dinner!" The red-eyed beast bared his teeth and growled.

"Shit!" Julianne squealed. Her horse agreed and reared back on two legs with a high-pitched whinnie, almost kicking Julianne in the head in its distress.

The remnant took advantage of her distraction and lunged forward. Julianne grabbed at the bridle, fending off her attacker with a clumsy kick. The remnant barked a short laugh and tried again.

This time, she was ready. The big, white horse came down, eyes wide and flank twitching. Julianne, now able to use the slack in the reins to move more freely, met her attacker with an elbow jab to the face, followed by a swift punch to the gut.

It made little impact. Yellow, cracked nails clawed at her face and fetid breath washed over her as the remnant opened its mouth, trying to snap crooked teeth at her neck. The remnant's face brushed hers, and Julianne felt the greasy, white face paint it wore as it smeared onto her skin.

A pulse bounced through the air that could be felt more than heard. The remnant convulsed and coughed, blood-filled mouth spattering Julianne's face with warm liquid.

Squeezing her eyes shut, Julianne spat. "Ugh, that's disgusting." She dabbed her eyes with a sleeve and opened them again.

"Let me guess," Marcus said. "You could have taken him?"

"Don't be silly." Julianne patted the horse's neck, soothing him. "I was busy with old 'fraidy-pants here. What took you so long, anyway?"

"What… Gah!" Marcus threw up his hands and turned away, missing the glimmer of mirth in Julianne's eyes.

"Thank you, dear," she called after him. "And sorry for being a crotchety old woman earlier."

"And?" Marcus prompted.

"And?" Julianne repeated, not willing to give him too much ground.

Marcus sighed. "You're never going to admit I was right, are you?"

"Of course, I am," Julianne quipped. "As soon as you actually are right."

Marcus prodded the dead remnant with the toe of his boot. "What's he doing this far from the Madlands, anyway?"

Julianne shook her head worriedly. They were too close to Annie's for comfort. "Bastian said they'd been infesting the area, but I didn't realize they'd come this far. Did you see the face paint? It's not one of the Madlands pack members."

Marcus nodded. "Well, that's what we're here to fix." He left the still-warm corpse and mounted his horse. "Let's ride the rest of the way. I want to make sure these pricks haven't been bothering Annie."

Julianne nodded absentmindedly as she slid a hand into the deep pocket of her robe. Inside, her fingers brushed a small, round object, hard as stone and cold to her touch. She stroked it gently and felt it shudder, then unfurl.

Tiny claws clutched her middle fingertip, and a dry snout wrapped around it. "Sorry, little one. No treats just yet."

The tiny creature soon grew bored with the lack of offering from Julianne. It pulled away, wriggling around to wedge deeper into the cloth. A moment later it began the rhythmic, telltale shudder that signaled it was asleep.

CHAPTER TWO

Julianne rapped on the wooden door, fresh white paint glowing in the brightly-lit night. She rubbed her eyes as she waited for it to open. Behind her, Marcus shifted irritably.

"Hush," Julianne admonished. "And for Bitch's sake, wipe your feet before we go in?"

Marcus eyed his boots. Mud was caked around the edges of each sole, one of the boots sporting a smear up the toe where he'd tripped on a clod of dirt. His gaze slid to Julianne's pristine leather shoes. "Why are yours so clean?" he grumbled.

Julianne knocked again, this time smiling when a grumpy, "Hold your horses!" called from the other side.

"I cleaned them in the creek," she explained. "And then I *rode* through the swamp, instead of clomping through the mud like an idiot."

Marcus opened his mouth to protest—*she* had been the one who'd asked him to lead her horse through a particularly swampy field of grass—but he was cut off as the door swung open and hit the wall behind with a thump.

"I don't know what business you have at this time of night,

but—" Annie looked up, her eyes widening and words faltering as she recognized who stood on her tiny front porch. "Well, Bitch bless me!"

She slapped a hand to her mouth at the words. Annie wasn't one to take the Bitch's name like that, but damned if she wasn't shocked to her bones to see these two standing there.

"Annie!" Julianne leaned forward and wrapped the older woman in a tight embrace. "I've missed you!" she exclaimed. "How are the boys?"

Annie pushed Julianne back to look at her, eyes moist as she clucked over the travel stains on Julianne's pants. The one pair had lasted her the entire trip through the Madlands, and they showed the result of the gory fighting.

"Boys are just fine." Annie ushered them in, with only a cursory glare at Marcus's boots. Nevertheless, he slid them off and set them neatly outside the door before stepping inside. "Harlon's gone to work for Francis, you know. Some kind of secretary, he says. Both are doing well, thanks to you."

Julianne shook her head at Annie's beaming smile. "That has nothing to do with me," she said. "They're smart, capable men. Francis especially has a gift for working with people."

Annie couldn't argue with that, so she set about taking the couple's packs and piling them by the door. "You'll be staying the night, I presume? Too late to be traipsing into town."

"We'd hoped that would be ok," Julianne said gently. "But if it's too much bother—" Even Julianne's words faltered under the furious glare Annie gave them, as if the old woman were offended at the suggestion.

"Have you eaten? Of course not." She jabbed an elbow at Marcus. "I know the kind of food that one packs when he's going somewhere." Nodding, Annie bustled off to the kitchen.

"Hey," Marcus called. "Any soldier would be happy with my cooking!"

"You're not feeding a soldier," Annie snapped, sticking her head back around the corner and waving a tea-towel at him threateningly. "You're catering for a lady, and an important one at that!"

Marcus shrugged, grinning at Julianne. "Well, she's got me there."

Julianne shook her head and waved at the bags. "Go put them away and stop hassling the poor woman."

She wandered into the kitchen, where Annie was just sliding a square tin into the oven. White dough puffed out of the top, dusted by tiny black seeds. On the bench beside her, three trays of raw oat cookies were carefully laid out.

"Having a bake up?" Julianne asked, inhaling the comforting scent of cinnamon and apple as she perched on a stool.

Annie scowled. "Since the traders have stopped coming so often, things have been scarce. I thought I'd run these into town first thing tomorrow, see if it don't make a few smiles crop up amongst the gloom."

Julianne bit her lip, wincing. She'd come back to Tahn because of the strange portal, but knew that the recent increase in remnant numbers had harried the town in her absence. "How bad is it?" Julianne asked.

"Well…" Annie blushed, an uncharacteristic reaction that Julianne noted with surprise. "A few brave men still make their way down, and they've been good enough to make sure we're not wanting for anything urgent."

"Oh?" Julianne asked, itching to know what had flustered the other woman so badly, but unsure what question to ask to discover it.

Julianne's ability to read minds had no bearing here. Annie had not only been good to Julianne, she'd also been clear about her thoughts on reading minds uninvited. No mystic who had met her would intrude there without a damn good reason.

Thudding footsteps announced Marcus's return and he slipped into the kitchen with a grin. He leaned down to peck Annie on the cheek, then darted away from a flick of her tea towel.

"Don't you be getting fresh with me, young man," she scolded. Despite her words, her eyes twinkled happily. "The bread won't take long to cook. You both go and freshen up." Her eyes raked Julianne's blood-stained clothes with distaste.

"Thank you, Annie." Julianne slid off her chair but paused on her way out. "I have to attend a meeting. You know…" She tapped her temple to signify the meeting would take place in her mind. "I might be a bit late coming down."

"Get yourself dressed, then go make yourself comfortable on the back porch," Annie said. "There's no one here to bother you, and I'll do my best to make sure *this* one is too busy to get in your way."

Marcus lifted his hands. "I would never!"

"Fact remains, I need a man's strength to help me with some things. You're a man, if I guessed right?" Annie left the taunt hanging.

"All you had to do was ask." Marcus's face was painted with a wounded expression, but it was quickly followed by a grin when Annie rolled her eyes at him.

Julianne quickly ran upstairs to find her things stacked neatly on a bed. It was the same room Annie had put her up in last time she had been in Tahn. The bedsheets were smooth and neatly tucked, and despite holding the stale scent of a long-closed room, not a speck of dust marred the thin mantle over the tiny fireplace.

Apart from plain linen curtains and a small corner table, the room was undecorated. Julianne preferred it that way—it suited Annie's perfunctory, no-nonsense attitude.

Julianne fished the alien creature from her pocket. Uncurled, it was shaped like an almond—if almonds had long, straw-like snouts and flared ridges along each side.

The shell sparkled, a deep rust-red color that threw flecks of light onto the walls as she held it up to the sun. "I know, boy. It was a long trip, and you're hungry. We're nearly there, though. You can see your friends again!"

She had no idea if the little beasts had a social structure like bees or ants, or if they were solitary. She didn't even know if—or how—they mated. Her assumption that she held a boy was based on nothing more than a gut feeling, and the vague memory of a pet rat she'd had for a short time as a child.

With her free hand, she dug into one of her bags and pulled out a sheaf of paper. Tearing one off, she twirled it around. The creature shivered in anticipation, shrugged its shell over its head twice and let out a high-pitched whistle.

The paper jerked from her fingers, and trembled and vanished into a mouth hidden beneath the shell. As it ate, the creature warmed in her hand. Not enough, though—after a good feed, the little beast would heat to burning.

When the door creaked, Julianne jumped.

"It's just me, girl." Annie shouldered her way past the door holding a large pitcher and a bowl with a cloth draped over the side, all piled on top of a thick, folded towel. "Water's warm, but won't be for long." Setting the crockery on the table and the towel on the bed, she turned, then jumped back.

"Sorry, Annie." Julianne held the creature close. "I forgot to tell you—I've brought a friend."

"I'm well familiar with those little vermin," Annie said. "Ate my only copy of Tessa's scone recipe, they did."

"Oh, dear." Julianne frowned, feeling the tension in the air.

"It's not that I mind them, so much as I don't like them," Annie explained. "That's no beast of Irth, you mark my words. And that flaming doorway to nowhere your friend found? Nothing but trouble."

Julianne sighed. "I hope you're wrong, Annie. I really do. And I wish I could say I thought you were."

Annie nodded curtly. "You just keep that thing away from my kitchen. Long as it doesn't eat any more of my important notes, it can stay."

"Thanks, Annie." Julianne lifted it to her face and pursed her lips in a kiss. "You won't be any trouble, will you boy?"

Flicking an eyebrow high, Annie snorted. Then she stomped off downstairs, leaving Julianne to dress.

She set the little beast on the mantle, knowing from long nights watching it that it wouldn't fall off. As she expected, its little snout felt along the edge and it backed up a safe distance, then settled down to nap again.

Satisfied, Julianne set herself to getting ready. She poured a little water into the bowl and dipped her hands in, scrubbing them together. Then, she dipped the cloth in and carefully sponged off the worst of the travel-dirt and remnant stains.

It took some time, but when she was done it felt like she'd been given new skin. Her flesh now had a pink glow from the scrubbing, and despite a brisk toweling off, was still damp when she slipped her dress on.

The fabric clung and bunched up. By the time she'd wriggled it down past her hips, Julianne's face was flushed, and her hair had started to curl from the warmth of her skin.

After placing the portal-beast back safely in her pocket, she made her way downstairs. Marcus had one of Annie's windows on the ground and was fiddling with the hinges.

"Making yourself useful?" she asked.

"Well, I figured you'd be busy for a while," he replied. "May as well make myself at home."

"Good call." Annie was nowhere in sight, but when Julianne stepped out of the back door onto the small, tidy porch, a pot of tea and a finely painted cup sat ready for her.

She sank into an old white rocker and took a moment to

center herself. Steam drifted lazily from the spout of the tea pot, indicating it was still hot. Julianne watched the tendrils rise and twist, then vanish into the crisp evening air.

Blinking to bring herself back to the present, Julianne poured herself a cup and held it in both hands, letting the heat soak into her skin. Her eyes clouded over with a soft white glow as she reached out with her magic.

CHAPTER THREE

Margit? She sent the call across Irth, all the way back to the Mystic Temple on the other side of the Madlands.

The thought still filled her with wonder. Though she'd been using Artemis's device for a month to stay in contact with Bastian, the ability to 'speak' to those back in the Temple while she was gone... Well, it changed everything.

You're late, came Margit's brisk reply. *Run into trouble, did you?*

The blasted rains slowed us down, Julianne explained. *The ground was so soft even the horses were having trouble.*

But you're safe in Tahn?

Yes. Julianne sent a quick mental image of their arrival at Annie's, followed by one of her perched on the rocker by a hot cup of tea.

Margit quickly shot back a vision of her own predicament—sitting in Julianne's office, paperwork piled high beside her and a congealed plate of barely-touched food set off near the edge of the desk.

Watch out, girl, Margit said. *I might just waltz across the Madlands and join you, if these fool Mystics don't stop making work for me.*

Concerned, Julianne wondered what had gone wrong. *I made sure everything was up to date before I left!*

Bah, Jonsen has it in his head that everything needs to be double-annotated while you're gone and wants me to check the papers Artemis has been producing, too. Margit's distaste at the idea leaked through the thoughts she sent.

Tell him to stop. By direct order from me, if need be. Julianne felt Margit's mental eye-roll and added, *If he won't listen, hook him up to a device of his own, and I'll tell him my damned self.*

Margit snorted, the tone and inflection so perfect that Julianne knew she must have made the sound out loud. *That might even stop him. Silly old goat is petrified of the sight of his own blood—maybe that can be my threat of choice while you're gone.*

Julianne sent a wave of affection, laced with commiseration. The mystics were an odd bunch, and loyal to a fault, but in Julianne's absence they tended to make everything into a drama.

As much as I'd like to reminisce about Jonsen's frustrating attention to detail, Julianne sent, ignoring a second snorting impression from Margit, *We have things to discuss.*

That we do, Margit sent, voice resigned. *Will you go first? I don't expect you have much to share.*

We were attacked by a roving remnant well beyond the Madlands, Julianne sent flatly. *Just the one—it was either separated from its pack or had abandoned them.*

Or been abandoned by them, Margit pointed out. *They're not exactly known for their strong family ties, after all.*

Fair point, Julianne conceded. *But still, this was a little far out for my comfort. The beast wasn't from the Mads, I don't think.*

How can you tell? Margit's interest was caught, now, and her thoughts were soaked with curiosity.

Julianne took a sip of her tea, and grimaced when she realized it was already starting to go cold. It was a common problem. Always busy, always distracted. Still, she enjoyed the adrenaline coursing through her as she faced this new problem.

It had white marks painted on its face, like the creatures we saw who claimed Chet as their leader. That was a story that had fascinated the mystics when she'd told them. Remnant rarely claimed a leader for more than a raid or three.

Margit didn't respond immediately, going quiet for a moment to think over the ramifications. *If remnant had indeed travelled all the way across the marshy forest toward a rival group, something must be driving them.*

Do you mind if I pull Amelia and our Tahn contingent in? Julianne asked. *I still haven't told Bastian I'm back yet.*

Oh, go ahead, Margit sent comfortably. *The boy will be knocking on my mind any minute now.*

Oh? Margit hadn't mentioned that earlier.

Yes, she sent wryly. *Every afternoon, checks in like clockwork to see if you've reached your checkpoint.*

Why doesn't he ask me himself? Julianne wondered.

Doesn't want to bother you, I imagine.

Shaking her head, Julianne reached out to Bastian and Amelia, twin tendrils of magic stretching across the world thanks to the amphorald at her wrist.

They both answered immediately, Amelia with a buoyant excitement and Bastian with a rush of relief.

Julianne! Amelia sent. *I'm so glad to hear from you. Are you really so far away?* Her thoughts had the same eagerness as Julianne's had the first time she used the communication device.

I am, Julianne replied, reflecting the other woman's wonder. *Isn't it amazing?*

You arrived safely? Bastian sent.

More or less, Julianne thought back, making sure to keep her communication open to all three of them. *Bastian, have the townspeople complained of any remnant attacks out this far? I ran in to one just past Annie's.*

Startled alarm suggested he hadn't. *We'll need to set patrols to circle the whole town.* Worry flickered at the edge of his thoughts, now. *I don't know how much farther Bette can stretch her men, though.*

I'm desperately short of soldiers myself, Amelia broke in, *but let me know if the situation is desperate, and I'll see what I can do.*

Gratitude suffused their bond, from both Julianne and Bastian. *We can discuss that with Francis later today,* Julianne said. *Amelia, you're an absolute gem. Margit, do you have any updates?*

There was a pause, and Julianne imagined the older mystic shuffling papers. *The first crate of communication devices arrived from the rearick. Found out why that bastard Tavich took so long—he made the damn things look pretty!*

Julianne had to hide a wry appreciation for the old man's tactics. Julianne had ordered over two-hundred of Artemis's communication devices, and they were to be delivered in staggered lots over the next two years.

Though she hadn't explained their use to Tavich, he would know the mystics would wear them—and that meant they would be seen. Nothing less than the very best could be associated with rearick crafting, so Tavich had made sure that fine details and quality work would be clearly visible.

Julianne rubbed her own bracelet. The gem was the one Artemis had used, but it was reset into a heavier strap with an ornate surround. It would easily pass as a simple piece of jewelry —something Julianne had insisted on.

She didn't intend to keep the communication devices a secret, specifically, but the mystics were, in general, a mysterious bunch. Julianne certainly wouldn't be advertising their new ability to communicate across Irth, and she didn't think anyone else would, either.

Let them be, she told Margit. *You know what the rearick are like. If you tell them to make the devices less detailed, they'll turn the blasted things into works of art.*

Silly old fools. The thought escaped Margit and echoed through the mental bonds they all shared. Julianne smiled at the sentiment. It was something Margit had been called more than once.

Bastian quickly filled the silence. *Did you manage to bring one for Danil, Master? He's been dying to try it.*

I did. Julianne shared a brief mental image of the bracelet she'd had made for her fellow mystic. *And I brought two more, in case they are needed this side of the Mads.* She had hoped for more, but could not afford to wait for the crafters to finish them.

We can discuss the bracelets later, Margit said pointedly. *Despite their valuable nature, I want to know what's going on at that portal.*

Has your research turned up anything new? Julianne asked her.

A resounding sense of frustration flooded her mind in reply. *These Bitch-forsaken records are so incomplete! Not a damned word about them. For all we know, they've never been seen before.*

Maybe they haven't, Julianne thought back. She was dubious about it—the Matriarch had traveled so far, seen so much that it seemed impossible for anything to occur that she hadn't experienced.

We've gone through what little information we have here, Amelia said. *There's no mention of strange creatures or portals.*

Julianne shrugged off the light disappointment she felt. No one had really expected to find the answer to what they were facing in their degraded, incomplete histories. *Bastian, any new developments?*

The arrivals have slowed. Just one in the last three days. Concern touched his thoughts about the small creatures like the one Julianne had adopted as a pet. *I don't know if that's a good thing or a bad one.*

Do you have a total count?

A scatter of numbers crossed her mind as Bastian's mental calculations leaked through the bond. *I'd say... thirty or more?*

Julianne's eyebrows shot up. *That many?*

It's just a guess, but I don't think I'm far off. Of course, quite a few of those are dead—the remnant seem bent on wiping the poor things out.

17

Bastian's shudder of distaste made goosebumps run over Julianne's skin.

Absentmindedly, she reached into her pocket to stroke the little creature inside. It was curled up tight, probably in response to her use of magic. Every time she'd cast a spell or used mental communication, the little beast had skittered away or wrapped itself into an impenetrable ball.

The increased remnant activity is certainly a worry, Julianne said. *But, I wish there was a way to stem the flow of incoming... whatever they are. At least until we work out what they are.*

You think they're dangerous? Bastian asked dubiously.

Worry twisted Julianne's gut. Though the small things had so far caused no more trouble than a few eaten bits of paper, her mind was weighed down with the possibilities—more of them, in plague numbers; larger beasts, more destructive than their tiny kin; or, something else entirely.

No one knew what lay on the other side of the portal. It could be a fiery hell, or paradise lost. It could harbor all manner of creatures, and likely not all would be as friendly as their little companions had been so far.

Amelia saved Julianne from sharing her fears. *Bastian, until we know without a doubt what these things are and where they are from, we can't say how dangerous they might be.*

Fair enough. Bastian almost managed to hide the reluctance in his voice, but Julianne wasn't fooled. She knew the younger man wanted the portal to become a beacon of hope and progress. Julianne wished she were still that naive.

Bastian, I know you want this to turn out to be a good thing, a new frontier. Julianne filled the words with warmth, then added an edge to them. *But we have no idea what's out there. Remember, Bethany Anne left Irth to face threats we can't even imagine.*

That was hundreds of years ago! he protested, though a trace of disappointment in his thoughts showed the warning had begun to sink in.

And she was, as far as we can tell, immortal. If she'd beaten the threat, would she not have come back? Julianne waited, letting the heavy silence stand for a moment. *Of course, the very fact that we don't know anything about these portals means I could be completely wrong. Just... don't do anything crazy, ok?*

Of course, Master. I'm not Danil. A cheeky mirth crept back into Bastian's thoughts, and Julianne shook her head wryly.

And thank the Bitch for that, Margit interjected. *Not even a mystic could put up with two of him.*

Margit! Julianne admonished. *Amelia, I'm sorry for this lot.*

Amelia's humor flooded Julianne's mind. *Oh, I don't mind a bit. It's a welcome distraction.*

Julianne's brows furrowed. *Distraction? Is everything ok in Arcadia?*

It's still difficult, but things have gotten much better. The economy is growing, especially with the governor of Cella on our side. He has been training up the Arcadian Guard. We are low on well-trained guards at the moment, but that changes every day. There is still so much work to be done, but Arryn destroyed what was left of Adrien's rule. In a few months, I think we will be ready for anything.

Is she still around? Julianne asked with curiosity. That wasn't the first time Amelia had mentioned the girl's name.

There was a sense of pride and humor in Amelia's thoughts. *The last I heard, they had won their battle and were heading south to deal with the bandit problem that's plagued the Valley. Unfortunately, I believe she and the others are in for a journey much like yours after that. Two young women came from a place called Kemet searching for help, and I sent them in Arryn's direction.*

Julianne thought about that for a few moments. *So, the problem is wide-spread. Interesting.*

It seems so, Amelia replied. *They spoke of a large portal and monsters plaguing their lands. From the sound of it, it gets worse every day. If I'm honest, a lot of time has passed. I'm unsure if they will even have a home to return to. But I have faith in Arryn. Just like I have faith in Hannah and faith in you. Though I can't be there with you, I will certainly do all I can to aid you along the way.*

Thank you, Amelia. Perhaps one of these days we can sit and reflect on all of our successes over a cup of tea or brew and not have to discuss the future plans for war. She sighed, then continued. *I hate to cut this short, but I really need to go,* Julianne admitted. *We almost rode straight through the Madlands—Marcus wouldn't stop for more than a few hours at a time, and I'm exhausted.*

I heard the noise you two were making in the wee hours every morning you were here, Margit huffed. *Don't pretend you're not used to missing a bit of sleep in favor of spending time with your man.*

Margit! Julianne had to concentrate to block her embarrassment leaking through the mental link. If Margit saw that, she'd never let the matter drop. *We were training. To fight!*

Is that what the kids call it now? Margit's tone was sweet enough to make sugared sweets taste like lemons.

Goodnight, Margit. Julianne promptly dropped her connection to the older mystic. *You too, Bastian. I'll see you in the morning.* She let him fall away too, leaving her link to Amelia until last.

Jules... how much of a threat are we facing, really? With knowing where Arryn is heading, and now you, too... I feel more and more claustrophobic every day being stuck here and unable to help. The deeply-etched worry of a leader facing an endless battle colored Amelia's thoughts.

Julianne's heart ached, knowing that if she dropped her shields just a little, the same fears for her people would be mirrored back to the Arcadian Governor. *I wish I knew, Amelia.*

CHAPTER FOUR

Bette shifted her feet, altering her stance a little. She crouched low, clenching her muscles.

Garrett watched appreciatively. *It'd take a Bitch-damned battering ram to shift the lass now,* he mused. *And even then, me money'd be on her.*

The rapid, nervous breath of a nearby soldier reminded him why Bette was bracing herself, and he quickly dropped low and hefted his axe. A quick glance around showed him the team was ready.

The six Tahn guardsmen flanked Bette, weapons ready, beads of sweat pearling on their upper lips and foreheads as they faced the impossible.

Twelve feet away, a bolt of frozen lightning hung in the air. Not a white flash, but a crooked black cut in reality, a thin sliver of space that led to another world.

The dark crack sucked light in, absorbing it into a deep chasm that was paper-thin, yet deep as an ocean. As Garrett watched, the edges warped and billowed, wavering like smoke.

"Aye, beastie. Come out, come out, wherever ye be." He

grinned at Bette's scowl. She hated it when he made light of the situation.

"I told ye not ta do that," she snapped.

"Ye told me I wasn't allowed ta tell it ta 'push, woman, push!'. Ye said nothing about callin' the wee beasts out."

Reality shuddered. With a twist and a pop, someone fell out of the crack in the air. No, not someone. Some*thing*.

"What the fuck is this?" Garrett's face creased in bewilderment. "He's not one of our wee beasties. He's a… What is he?"

The beast was bigger than the ones that had come through before, and seemingly more alert. It stood on four roach-like legs, and though its long snout hung limp, its beady eyes protruded from fat humps in the scaly face.

Those eyes darted around, quickly shifting back and forth as it rocked back onto its hind legs. Forelegs rose up to paw the air, stretching over the creature's total height of just over a foot.

"He's a fuckin' monster, like the rest of them." Carey spat on the ground. "Sharne'll have my balls for this. She always said there was more beyond that crack."

"Crack? More like a giant vagina, spittin' out baby monsters from hell." Mack relaxed his grip on the long spear. "And Sharne's wrath will be worth it, just to see the look on Danil's face when we tell him he missed this."

Carey shifted warily. "It's not *acting* like it wants to bite our faces off. You think he's friendly, like the others?"

"Boy, they're about as friendly as slugs. And pests, too." Sherp shook his head. "You should see what they did to my books."

"Porn ain't books." Garrett said it deadpan, refusing to display the glint in his eye. "And it's better off gone. Maybe ye'll find yerself a real lass, now?"

"Shut your face, they were quality girls, you sperm-swilling—what the fuck?" Sherp jerked backwards in fright.

The conversation ceased as the creature from the rift scuttled up a tree. It eyed the men the whole time, pudgy neck forming rolls as it twisted to watch them as it ran.

Garrett jumped as a screech rang out from the bushes behind him. "ATTACK!" he bellowed. "REMNANT!"

Remnant were indeed attacking, but not them. Three of the fetid beasts burst out of the dense foliage and swarmed up the tree the creature had climbed, jumping to catch branches and scraping toes on the rough bark as they climbed.

"Get the bastards!" Bette yelled and launched herself forwards. She stabbed her sword through the calf of a disappearing remnant, pinning it to the tree, howling.

Bette thumped the sword to hold it firm, then drew a dagger. "To the trees, ye gutter-licking pricks! Garrett?"

She dropped her stance to prepare to run, and Garrett's eyes widened. He spun, dropped to a knee and crouched just in time for her to leap onto his back. He shoved upwards, flinging her towards a sturdy branch.

"And how the fuck am I supposed to get up there?" he called as she hoisted herself up and ran towards the center of the tree.

"Climb, ye lazy turd." She darted around a thick trunk, dancing from branch to branch, making her way towards the two remnant some distance away.

Garrett looked around in desperation. His comrades were already scaling fat trunks and swinging from limbs. "Never thought I'd say this but... I'm too fucking short!"

All the routes leading up were out of his reach, and his strong legs were designed for kicking, not jumping.

Rather than dwell on his inadequacy, he bolted through the undergrowth, one eye towards the battle waging above.

The remnant had cornered the portal beast, which clung to the wobbling tip of a thin branch. It had nowhere to go but down —a drop far enough to make even Garrett's sturdy stomach do a backflip.

One of the remnant slid a foot out, grinning when the branch held.

"Leave the wee bastard alone, ye moldy scab-knuckles!" Garrett yelled. He stepped back a little, allowing him a better view.

He reached one hand behind his back as he spoke, eye locked on the scene above. With a smooth movement, a small throwing axe dropped into his grasp.

"You're dumb as rocks!" the remnant shrieked. "Kill the destroyers!" It hurled itself forward as Garrett flicked his arm up, hurling the sharp-bladed weapon into the trees.

The axe struck home, lodging in the remnant's arm, the momentum throwing it off the branch. A sickening moment later, the remnant landed with a muffled crunch.

"Bette!" Garrett yelled. "Get yer ass over—"

He hadn't noticed her sneaking up on the second remnant, hidden behind the trunk of a tree. She jumped, tackling her opponent and knocking it off balance. Her legs wrapped around it as they tumbled, rolling off the precarious platform.

Garrett's heart stopped, lurching again when Bette slammed her own throwing axe into the branch. She dangled, and the remnant dangled with her, gnashing and snarling as it tried to pull itself up her leg.

She kicked and twisted, and the remnant fell, its life ending as abruptly as its loud shriek.

Bette hoisted herself back up to the branch, and Garrett's chest finally billowed with a deep breath. She grinned down at him.

"What? Ye didn't think I'd fall, did ye?"

Garrett just shook his head. Then, he frowned, squinting. "What's that on yer face?" he asked. A dark splotch had appeared and now slid down her face, leaving a long streak.

Bette touched it and pulled her hand away, face drawing tight in concern. She looked up.

Garrett followed her glance, just in time to see the remnant that had been left pinned to the tree as it fell with outstretched arms from a branch high above Bette and the portal beast.

Like a graceful bird, the remnant slipped silently through the leaves and branches. Garrett couldn't move, couldn't breathe.

The absurdity of it had taken his senses, left him unable to react as the remnant ploughed past the portal beast, latching onto one of its legs and pulling it down in a suicidal dive.

They met the ground together, the thick sound of two bodies slamming onto hard dirt and soft leaves vibrating through Garrett like a painful heartbeat.

Silence fell, cut by a furious shriek from above.

"Fuck!" Bette hurled her axe in anger, slamming it down to cut a path through the leaves and losing it in a branch below. "Fuck."

Her second curse was subdued.

Garrett's brow furrowed, unsure why the death of a strange beast from a stranger land cut so deeply. Hell, they might have had to kill it themselves, eventually.

He pushed through a cluster of vines and approached the splattered mess. Blood streaked his sleeve as he pushed through a bush and more squelched beneath his boots as he approached.

The remnant and the portal beast had combined, broken bodies intermingled, bones and flesh and carapace pulverized by the force of the fall.

"That smells like a moldy goat carcass covered in week-old shit," Garrett muttered, covering his face with the front of his shirt.

He swallowed, glad his shift had started too early to eat before.

"I think I just lost all desire for lunch." Mack stepped forwards, peeked at the carnage, then looked away. His green face faded to a grey pallor.

"What, ye don't wanna snack on that?" Garrett asked with an

evil grin. "Here. I'll scoop some up, and ye can take it home for dinner. It'll have time to ferment a bit by then."

He let out a deep belly laugh as Mack pressed his lips together, swayed, then ran off into the forest. The sound of his retching almost made Garrett do the same, but it was worth the discomfort.

"Yer a wee bit soft in the guts, lad!" Garrett called after him. "Need ta toughen up if ye want ta be in the business of killin' things!"

"Yer a right donkey's ass," Bette opined as she stomped towards him. "Don't think I didn't hear ye."

"Aye, well. We need a bit of fun now and then." Garrett looked down, feigning a chastened expression.

Bette rolled her eyes. "Ye don't fool me, ye salty old goat's testicle."

"What exactly do ye think it was?" Garrett asked, sobering as he saw a broken, spiked leg poking out from the fleshy mess.

Bette shrugged. "The wee thing didn't *seem* to want to cause any harm, though he was a bit more awake than the wee-er ones we've seen so far."

"It didn't have a chance, did it?" Bile swirled in Garrett's stomach again as a fresh breeze pushed the stench of shit and coppery blood towards his nostrils.

"Aye. But… I dunno, it looked more scared than homicidal, ye know?"

She prodded a lumpy gibbett of flesh with the toe of her boot, much to Garrett's roiling disgust. When she squatted down to poke it with her knife, he gave up.

"Bitch," he mumbled in a strangled voice as he turned and vomited bile into a nearby bush.

"Who's soft in the guts now?" she asked with an evil cackle.

CHAPTER FIVE

"Drop it, now! No, you mouth-breathing moron! *DROP!*" Jessop gestured with his hands and finally, the men manning the makeshift winch lowered the enormous post into the hole.

Bastian sighed in relief. The old man directing the event stomped over to him, shaking his head.

"Bunch of soft-skirted idiots. You'd think they'd never even built a barn before." Jessop sucked his teeth and rubbed a thin sheen of sweat from his forehead.

"To be fair, this is a little more involved than a regular barn," Bastian said. He flinched as the distant sound of fighting drifted past the pause in work.

Jessop frowned. "Looks like those damned remnant are at it again." He spat on the ground. "Can't say that I'd have the potatoes to be building a new home so close by that rip in the world." He grabbed his crotch to make sure Bastian understood.

The mystic gave a quick, nervous grin. "Bette won't let them past."

Jessop nodded. "Still. There's only two of those rearick and a handful of fighters with them. Wouldn't take much for some hellspawned demon to slip through that hole and come for us."

Bastian swallowed, hard. "The bugs? They're tiny. They haven't hurt anyone yet."

Jessop laughed. "Nothing does, until it does. Next thing you know, you're short one leg and two pints of blood, and your team is strung up by their eggs by the enemy."

"Jessop, how many euphemisms for balls do you actually know?" Bastian asked, the question pressing harder than his worry. "Because I've counted four today, not including the time you called Mack a pile of wet vaginas."

Jessop frowned, then raised both hands. He quickly ticked off all ten fingers on both, then again. Midway through the third round, he paused. "Uhh… I've lost count."

Bastain laughed. "I thought so. Now, where's that schematic for the hall?" He looked around, then let out a yelp and a curse.

"Oi!" Jessop yelled, seeing the small red creature on Bastian's makeshift workbench. "Get off, you rock-brained little sack of beans." He paused as Bastian raced over to pull a soggy drawing from the creature's mouth. "Hey, that was number twenty-seven!"

Bastian grabbed the little beast, then promptly dropped it and shook his singed fingers. Still, he managed to free the paper—or, what was left of it.

Bastian growled and held up the mangled schematic. "Bitch-damnit!" He scowled at the tightly-coiled ball on the table. He slipped his hand inside his sleeve to protect his fingers. He hefted the creature in one hand, raised it over his shoulder…. then sighed and gently lowered it to the ground.

"Should have thrown the nasty little vermin," Jessop said, shaking his head. He sucked a whistle through his teeth again. "I keep saying, they're trouble."

"I know, I know," Bastian grumbled as he set the little creature on the dirt and nudged it with his toe.

It didn't move. Sighing irritably, he tore a strip off the paper he'd rescued—it was ruined anyway—and dangled it in front of the red ball.

It twitched. Then, it slowly unfurled to reveal beady little eyes and a long, trembling snout. Just before that snout shot forwards, Bastian snatched the paper out of its reach.

"Pig," he said. "Going by that heat you're putting out, you've clearly been eating all day."

The creature ambled forwards. Bastian moved, too. He painstakingly led it off towards a bush that had been damaged by the construction work. *Those dead leaves should keep the little beast busy for a while*, he thought to himself.

"As many phrases as I've got for a set of brass eggs, I've got none for a man as soft as you," Jessop said with a chuckle.

Bastian spared him a withering look. "We don't know what they are. Maybe they're lost, or somehow important."

"Your doorknockers are important, too. What if one of those critters sneaks into your bed and chews one off? You just can't trust a beast that looks like it belongs down a man's pants." Jessop nodded once to punctuate his words, then walked over to the workbench. "Should be another one of those plans in here somewhere."

Bastian let Jessop rummage through the papers, rubbing his head as he squinted into the morning glare.

"You look miserable, Mystic!" Tomas asked as he wandered past, a bucket of wet plaster balancing on a stick on his shoulder. "Tansy finally leave you for Mack?"

"He couldn't hold onto her for a night, let alone a relationship," Bastian scoffed.

"Ha!" Tansy's voice was bright and clear over the lower grumbles of conversation throughout the worksite. "He couldn't catch me in the first place, let alone hold on."

Tomas laughed and sauntered off, but Bastian's mind was already skipping across the long, long list of things he had to do.

He took a moment to re-center himself. His eyes glowed softly as he sank into a deep meditation, years of practice making the transition as easy as breathing.

Around him, sounds flitted past, ethereal and disconnected, yet part of a bigger symphony. The hum of voices ebbed and flowed, rustling leaves drowning out any silence in between gaps in conversation.

The faint scent of lavender tickled his nose, a heady aroma beneath the grounding smell of freshly turned dirt and the spice of newly-cut timber.

Bastian?

Amelia's thought floated into Bastian's mind, not interrupting his peace but gently bringing his mind back to the present.

Governor? What may I do for you? he replied.

I just wanted to give you a heads up. There's a trade wagon headed to Tahn, and with it will be two Arcadian-trained physical mages who are interested in seeing your school, or your plans for it, at least. The governor's tone was bland, but Bastian's heart raced.

Why so soon? He queried. *I'm far from ready.*

Word travels fast, she said with a hint of mirth in her thoughts. *And once these little trinkets start being handed out, it will go faster. Both of your guests are considering sending children there, if you impress them, and one is also interested in a teaching job.*

A barrage of images and thoughts flooded Bastian's mind. The two Arcadian women were both well-dressed. Tamara, a dark-haired woman with a stern, scowling face, had teaching credentials from Arcadia as well as experience running a small estate outside of the city.

Angelica was a plump, smiling woman with tightly curled blonde hair. A widow, she had arrived after three years in her husband's manor to the south.

Bastian felt, rather than saw the woman's doting attention on her two boys and didn't miss Amelia's slightly irritated reaction to her babying of them.

Importantly, neither woman had been a supporter of Adrien. Though they hadn't fought for the rebellion, either, both expressed goodwill towards the new policies Amelia had implemented.

Catching his relief at that, Amelia sent a mental chuckle. *You didn't think I'd let some stuck up noble come and teach for you, did you?*

Well, it would *be a handy way to get them out of the city,* Bastian admitted. Then, with an evil grin, he added, *And you know people have a tendency to go missing in the Madlands, right?*

I wish! The governor's attention faltered for a moment. *Sorry, Bastian. Someone just accidentally let off a fireball in the middle of breakfast. Gotta run!*

Very funny, Bastian sent. When Amelia didn't answer, he frowned. If she hadn't been joking…

Not for the first time in recent weeks, Bastian wondered if he really knew what he was in for. Oh, sure, he'd studied at the Temple—in a place where everyone knew each other's thoughts, and initiates were well aware of what was acceptable horsing around and what was a step too far.

But in a school with mixed modalities, where some of the teachers wouldn't even know mental magic, how would the students be held in line?

"Finished daydreaming?" Jessop asked patiently.

"Sorry," Bastian murmured. "I was just chatting to Amelia."

"Amelia? She's another one of your temple friends?" Jessop held two squares of paper up, slightly overlapping.

"Not exactly," Bastian said. "She—wait, is that a complete schematic?" The sheafs Jessop clutched matched up fairly well, and Bastian was sure Francis could fill in the details of the room that was chopped in half.

"Best you go get some copies of these," Jessop said. "I know enough to keep this lot busy, but once we get to the staircase, I'll need those measurements."

Bastian nodded curtly, then looked around. He waved an arm at Tansy. "Care for a wander back to town?" he called.

With a lazy step, she dropped off the beam she was balanced on. Bastian's heart lurched, but she caught herself, grabbing it with her hand and swinging safely to the ground. "Sure. *Someone* has to make sure you don't trip over your own feet."

CHAPTER SIX

Julianne leaned back in her chair, rubbing her stomach. "I haven't eaten this much since last time I was here," she said. "Tahn really knows how to put on a breakfast."

Francis smiled. "Our supplies are scant in some respects, but our local goods are second to none."

"I'd believe that," Marcus said, then let out a loud burp. "Sorry, Jules." He grinned.

"Bullshit you are," she grumbled. "That smells like sausages, you pig. Francis, before we started eating, you mentioned something about Danil not settling in?"

"Oh, he's happy enough while he's here," Francis said, blushing. "I didn't mean to imply otherwise."

"You may not have meant to, but you did." Julianne smiled. "You know I'll get it directly from him later, but I'd rather know what I'm in for."

Francis shrugged. "It's just that Polly is itching to leave. They both know it's safer here—I think that's what's got her feet so restless—but everyone can see they'll be glad once this portal business is sorted."

Julianne nodded. "Mystics are either perfectly happy in one spot, or absolutely miserable. I realized after we left that Danil had been bitten by the urge to go on a pilgrimage, so I'm not surprised he's eager to go."

Francis bowed his head, relieved that he hadn't given away some great secret. "Well, perhaps you could have a word with him? As much as we'd love him to stay and help, we don't need him, as such. I wouldn't want him to stay out of a sense of obligation."

Julianne laughed. "Obligation? You don't know Danil. It's pure curiosity keeping him here. He can't stand not knowing someone else's secret, especially if he's got money riding on it—I assume he has?" Her eyes twinkled, and she grinned when Francis nodded.

"I believe he has a hefty bag of coin wagered. He bet for the return of the Matriarch, I believe." Francis shrugged. "I suppose it's as likely an outcome as anything else... Except maybe Gerard's theory that it's all another mucker trick, and neither the creatures nor the portal really exist."

Julianne raised an eyebrow at that. "Any other theories I should know about?"

"Well... the leading theory is that they're beasts from beyond the stars, a species from another world. Danil's bet accepts that but adds on that their presence here signifies the return of Queen Bethany Anne. Mack thinks they're slipping through from the world of dreams, and Harlon put money on the chance of them being from another time."

Julianne shook her head. "I wish we knew with certainty, but if I hadn't learned from Danil never to place a bet against him, I'd run with the stars theory. Though our research so far doesn't give any weight to that theory, apart from the stories of Bethany Anne's departure."

There was one man who might know—Ezekiel. She had sent a group of mystics to seek him out, but knew it was a long shot.

He'd left in that ridiculous flying device Adrien had built, and could be halfway across Irth by now, if not flying out to the stars themselves.

If only we'd discovered the amphorald devices before he'd left, she mused. Apart from the pressing issues they faced, Julianne was also filled with curiosity about Hannah, the young magician Ezekiel had rescued and taken with him.

Bringing her thoughts back to the present, she asked Francis how the townspeople felt about the strange incursion.

"Well, the creatures don't seem to be more than a nuisance," he said.

As if on cue, Julianne's tiny companion wriggled in her pocket and tested the air with a skinny snout. With a clumsy heave, it pulled itself up, tumbling out of her pocket too fast for her to react. It tumbled onto the floor, wrapped itself into a ball before it landed, and stayed that way afterwards.

Francis snorted. "And it's not as if they seem to have the aptitude for a full-scale invasion."

Julianne bit her lip, then scooped up the spherical beast and nestled it safely in her lap, one hand cupping it in case it tried to scurry away again. Its well-fed warmth tingled on her fingertips.

"They don't," she said. "But what if there's something else out there, waiting to come through?"

Francis sobered. "That's why we've got the elite guard out watching the portal."

Julianne cocked an eyebrow, gesturing for him to explain.

"Bette and Garrett are leading them—Sharne has taken over the town guard. They've got a few of their best fighters out there, in case something does force its way through." Francis raised a finger in warning. "Everyone thinks they're just there because of the remnant. I'd rather the idea of more monsters out there stay amongst us, if that's ok."

"Wise idea," Julianne murmured. "Though I personally think the remnant are the bigger threat now, anyway."

"Yes." Francis ran a hand through his hair. "Garrett is sure the portal is pulling them closer, but I don't see that pattern myself. From what snippets the remnant have actually told us, intentionally or not, it seems they're just displaced."

"And the attacks on these guys?" she asked, gesturing to the one in her lap that was just starting to unfurl. She rubbed its belly with a finger, and it stretched lazily.

"Remember what Bastian said? About the monsters attacking that 'Chet' fellow and his horde?" Francis drummed his fingers on the arm of his chair nervously. "I wonder if they weren't right. If some beast came through and attacked, and they recognize these little critters as being linked to the same event…"

"You think the remnant are *scared* of them?" Julianne asked dubiously.

Francis shrugged. "Portals to the stars? Traveling through time? The Queen returning? Tell me my theory sounds crazier than any of those."

"You're right," Julianne said. "In fact, you're making the most sense of anyone so far." Frustration building, she let out a soft curse. "If only we knew more."

There was a loud knock at the door, and the tiny creature Julianne held snapped shut, catching her finger as it rolled into its protective shell.

"Ow!" she yelped, holding up her hand to view the dangling, cracked ball hanging from it. "Could you not do that?" Julianne begged. Grabbing it with her other hand, she squeezed her eyes shut and yanked, pulling her finger free but leaving a thin layer of skin behind.

Francis stood and hurried to the door, glancing over his shoulder at the injured mystic. "And here I thought they aren't dangerous."

"Only if you're stupid enough to get your finger stuck inside one," Julianne sighed, examining the damage. Thin lines of blood beaded along her finger, which was red and puffy.

She wiggled it carefully. "At least it's not broken."

"Jules!" Bastian peeked his head in as Francis swung the door back. "Master, it's so good to see you!"

She stood and embraced her former pupil, marveling at how much he'd changed since they'd started their journey together. No longer a hesitant young man, Bastian wore the confidence of a leader and the mental strength of one who had seen war.

Though she mourned the loss of his innocence, she was proud of his accomplishments and his ambition, and she let the emotion flood towards him through a light mental touch.

Bastian grinned, then grimaced. "Don't expect too much from a man stupid enough to let his schematics get eaten," he said, flashing an apologetic look at Francis.

"Again?" Francis chuckled. "Lucky I thought ahead."

Francis stepped over to a cupboard and slipped a key into a hole below the handle. He opened it, catching a handful of papers that flew out. The cupboard was stuffed to the brim with stacks of paper.

The bundle in Julianne's lap suddenly clicked open, snout sniffing the air.

"Oh, no you don't." She grappled it by the back shell, picking it up and letting it scrabble in the air with its tiny legs.

"Is that the one you took to the Temple?" Bastian asked.

She nodded. "It's been on one hell of a journey," she confirmed. "Though perhaps not as big as the one that brought it here."

Francis held out a large drawing to Bastian. "You're a genius and a lifesaver, Lord Francis."

Francis grinned. "No, I've just lost too damn many things to those vermin."

"At least they're cute?" Bastian said, examining the one Julianne held. He drew back when its snout made a grab for his plans. "What's his name?"

"Name?" Julianne asked, confused. "They don't talk, Bastian. Do they?"

"No," Bastian laughed. "I mean, what did you name it. You did give it one, didn't you?"

She shook her head, perplexed. "Why would I do that?"

Bastian erupted into a deep belly laugh. "You're keeping it as a pet, Jules! You tickle its belly—Don't deny it, it slips through the mental link all the time—and you feed it and carry it in your pocket. What is it with you and naming things?"

Julianne shrugged, contemplating the little animal she really had grown to care about. "I never had a pet as a child. I've never really been around animals at all, in fact, unless you count the horses I borrowed to travel."

"You're hopeless," Bastian laughed, shaking his head.

Julianne scowled indignantly. "Fine! You name him." She folded her arms expectantly.

"Ardie." Bastian threw out the name without hesitation.

"What?" Julianne dropped her arms, bewildered. "How did you come up with that so fast?"

Bastian shrugged. "Remember back at the Temple, in the records, we had those little books with hard pages?"

"You mean the children's books with the pictures?" Julianne asked, wrinkling her face as she stretched her memory.

Despite her many hours spent in those rooms, digging through books and literature, shuffling through records to find any mention of strange portals cracking the sky, or incursions of even stranger creatures, *that* particular pile of books had never been in her sights.

"Bastian…" She looked up, eyes wide. "Are you saying you *saw* these creatures in one of those books?"

He chuckled and shook his head. Julianne sank back into her chair, deflated.

"No," Bastian confirmed. "Not these. But Irth used to have an animal that reminds me of them. They've got shells like armour, and long noses. But they weren't red, and the back carapace was different."

Julianne reflexively ran a finger over Ardie's back. It was smooth and hard, a material that by rights, shouldn't have the ability to flex and bend as the creature moved, let alone seal up into a seamless sphere when it was scared.

"So, these... Ardies?"

"Aaaard-varks." Bastian spat the word out clumsily, tripping over the pronunciation of a name he'd never heard spoken, only read.

Julianne lifted her hands and narrowed her eyes, searching the beady, black spots looking back at her. "Ardie?" she said, gently.

Ardie snorted and rolled back up into a ball.

Julianne knocked on the hard, round shell. "Well, unless you come up with something better, you're stuck with it."

"What do we call them, then," Francis asked. "The creature name, I mean. They can't all be Ardies."

"Ardie the Vark," Marcus said laughing. "I guess Francis is right. We've discovered a new animal. It will need a name."

"Vark works fine for me," Bastian said. "What about you, Ardie? Are you a vark?"

A thin, fleshy rope snuck out of an opening that formed in the ball. It nuzzled Julianne's finger, then latched onto a fresh bit of paper she dangled before it. Snatching it back through the crack, it snapped shut.

"He seems ok with it." Julianne patted the protective shield and slipped it back into her pocket. She felt the warmth on her leg as the creature's digestive system kicked into gear.

"I swear you pay that thing more attention than you do to me," Marcus said from across the table.

"That's because Ardie is better looking," Bastian shot back.

Marcus turned to Julianne, face beseeching.

"Don't look at me," she said primly. "I agree with him!"

Wounded, Marcus settled back in his chair. "Stay single," he told Francis.

Francis just shrugged. "I'm not getting involved in this one. I'll lose an arm... or my mind. And quite frankly, I'd rather give up a limb."

"Speaking of minds," Bastian said, wrinkling his brow in thought. "Why do you think the druids can't reach these creatures?"

Julianne shook her head, sighing. "Mathias said maybe it's because they're not from around here. If a druid goes far enough away from their native area, their bond with the land gets weaker. It can take time to re-establish it."

"Well, maybe he'll have some answers when he comes back." Bastian rolled up the schematic and tapped it against his hand, thinking. "Jules... this is going to sound crazy, but you don't think they're somehow related to remnant?"

Julianne's eyebrows shot up. "Why would you say that?" She didn't point out the obvious—the creatures from the rift were, or at least seemed like animals. Remnant weren't quite human, but they were more than just beasts. She saw no reason for them to be connected.

Bastian blushed. "I tried to mind-read one. It didn't work, obviously—I'd have told you if it did. But, it wasn't the usually blank fuzz of an animal. I got... well, still static, but noisy static. I could see red, feel pain. It reminded me of our trip through the Mads, when Danil got his brain eaten by that remnant girl."

Julianne shuddered, thinking back to her dive into Danil's tortured mind. Those images had come as pain, smell, touch, and noise; disjointed sensations that weren't coherent but still made a wild kind of sense.

Julianne schooled her face, hiding her growing excitement. "Bastian, I absolutely forbid you to try that again. If there is some link between remnant and whatever is coming through that rift, connecting with them could be very dangerous."

Bastian nodded. "But you think there might be something to it?"

Julianne put her hands up. "We're in foreign waters here, Bastian. We can't rule anything out." She grinned. "But if *anyone* is going to try this... it has to be me."

"*What?*" Marcus and Bastian yelped at the same time. They looked at each other, mirrored images of concern.

Julianne snorted. "Come on. You think I'd let anyone else be the first to jump through this particular trap door?"

Bastian opened his mouth, but she snapped a hand up and cut him off. "Bastian, I'm not letting you risk yourself like that. And after what Danil went through when he used magic on that remnant, I'm not letting him anywhere *near* this idea."

"And I suppose you're invincible?" Marcus stood, hooking his thumbs through his belt. He stood in a dangerously relaxed pose, face calm.

Julianne recognized that stance. He'd used it at bars, and in the streets of Craigston during her recovery. Usually, it was during some drunk bully's rant about why he was entitled to punch a girl in the face, or walk out of Ophelia's without settling a bill.

And every time she'd seen it, it had ended in violence.

Julianne narrowed her eyes.

Marcus let a small smile touch his lips. He sank down further, looked more at ease and yet somehow, five times more dangerous.

"You wouldn't." Julianne's voice was just a shade uneven, and she swallowed, hoping he'd missed it.

"The pigs have been enjoying the weather, lately," he mused, flicking a glance out the window.

Her heart thumped once, a painful beat. There were no pigs in view, but Julianne recalled seeing three fat pigs wallowing in a giant mud pit on their way to see Francis.

Marcus turned to Bastian. "Bastian, how hard do you think it would be to hold a spell if you'd just been dumped on your ass in a cold, wet puddle of mud?"

"Pretty hard," Bastian said with a grin. That grin faded when Julianne shot him a dark look, but flashed again as Marcus continued.

"And, if a couple of pigs decided to start chewing your hair and licking your face?" Marcus's eyes shifted back to Julianne.

Julianne sighed. "You can't stop me, Marcus. Someone has to find out if this is possible."

"There's got to be another way," he said, not backing down. "Someone you can ask, who might know what these things are. Do you know where the Founder is?"

The beginnings of an idea flickered at the edges of Julianne's mind. "He's gone. Up north somewhere. But…" She trailed off, wondering if the idea was even worth trying.

It has to be at least as crazy as trying to get in the head of something even more distant than a remnant, she reminded herself.

At Bastian's questioning look, Julianne smiled. "But there may be a way to contact him. Maybe." She glanced at Bastian. "I'll need help, though?"

Bastian nodded eagerly. "Anything, Master."

"I'll hold you to that." Ignoring the sudden flicker of worry on her fellow mystic's face, Julianne stood. "We're all going to have a busy day. I suggest we get started."

She brushed past Marcus and Bastian, reaching for the doorknob. She hesitated, then suddenly ducked to one side as the door burst open.

"Lord Francis!"

The pink-faced girl in the doorway heaved heavy breaths and wiped sweat from her brow. She was young—maybe fourteen—and lithe, with the cocky posture of a seasoned performer.

"Yes, Clarke?"

"There's been another breach, and it's not like the others, but

Bette went after it, and a remnant got it first, and Garrett said to come, but Danil wanted to know first, so I have—"

"Stop!" Francis snapped.

Clarke's mouth snapped shut.

"Slow down, child. You said there was another breach?"

She nodded. "Yes, Lord Francis. But, it wasn't like our little tumblers."

Trying to stay up with the girl's excited story, Julianne brushed her mind. 'Tumblers' was a name the theatre troupe had given to the little creatures, due to their resemblance to the colored bronze spheres used in the circus acts.

Julianne plucked an image from her mind, muttered quietly, and deftly threw up an image for the room to see. A shimmering red bug sprawled on the ground, spiked legs twisted and face smashed into a pulp. It certainly wasn't a vark...

Clarke squealed in delight as Marcus and Francis gasped.

"That's it!" Clarke yelled. "That's exactly what I saw!"

Bastian looked on, somber. Julianne banished the image with a wave of her hand.

Marcus jerked to his feet. "We have to go help."

Clarke shook her head, still grinning. "Too late, soldier-boy. It's dead, and there won't be another one through for ages now. By the time you get there, Captain Bette and Lieutenant Garrett will be back in town, probably looking for you."

"Garrett seemed sure the remnant came for it," Julianne said, after sorting through Clarke's memories. "But... I don't know. I'd like to avoid making a judgement on that until I see it with my own eyes."

Marcus nodded. "The bastard we saw was in the wrong place to be headed towards the rift."

Francis rubbed his face. "If they're not coming for the rift, or the beasts that are coming through it... why the change? I've lived in Tahn all my life without seeing a remnant."

"What if they're not running to something?" Marcus asked quietly. "What if they're running *from* it?"

Julianne shuddered. Remnant were mindless, instinctual creatures that had, to her knowledge, never felt fear. Even when death stared them in the face, most would keep running towards it. What could scare a remnant who sought death?

CHAPTER SEVEN

Polly watched as Danil's eyes cleared. Once the white had faded, she could see the sparkling green color that was normally obscured.

His stance dropped. Knees bent, arms outstretched as if to feel the air, he slowly turned towards her.

Keeping her breath quiet, Polly stepped back, feet silent on the soft grass.

They had chosen this spot because Danil was getting too good. Senses heightened due to his blindness, it had gotten too easy for him to judge her position in the noisy undergrowth of the nearby forest.

Here, under the gentle sun and with a wide-open space to train in, it was harder for Danil to hear telltale movements as Polly moved in for the strike.

Come on, Danil, she thought. *You got this.*

She slid to the left, then darted forwards. Her blunt, wooden training sword whipped through empty air.

Danil laughed beside her. He'd twirled out of the way just in time.

"What gave me away?" she asked, grinning.

Danil's eyes shifted back to their usual white glow, much to Polly's disappointment. A tender caress on her mind brought her smile back, though, and she closed her own eyes to see what Danil wanted to tell her.

She concentrated on the sensations he sent through the bond. Warm sun, a gentle breeze. The easy flex of his muscles as he moved. The laser sharp concentration as he held onto every aspect of the world around him.

A touch of coolness fell over one arm. The breeze shifted. Danil spun.

"I don't understand," she said with a frown. "I was upwind of you, and you felt that—but you knew before then."

"Did you feel the shift in temperature?" he asked.

She nodded, but still couldn't put the pieces together.

Danil reached out and lifted her hand, stretching her arm out and pointing her palm to the sun. She could feel her skin warm even as the breeze whispered by.

He moved, standing so his shadow fell over her arm. It immediately cooled, the breeze taking on a crispness now that the sunshine wasn't there to offset it.

"My shadow!" she exclaimed. "I won't make that mistake again."

Danil pouted. "Every single time I find a new way to win, you use it against me. Why?"

Polly sobered. "One day, we'll be outside. You won't have your magic—maybe I won't be there. And maybe it'll be dark, or overcast, and there won't be dry leaves and snapping branches to rely on."

Danil sighed. "Ok. Fine. You've got a point, and I'll be damned if it's not a good one. Again?"

His eyes cleared, and Polly stepped back, careful to stay downwind and angling her shadow away from him.

The rapid beat of footsteps sounded nearby. Danil's eyes

flashed, and Polly swung, her rough weapon pointed towards the trail that led to the field.

Danil relaxed a moment before Polly. Then, his body tightened again. "Clarke!" he called. "Did they—I *missed it?*" Disappointment etched his features.

Clarke grinned. "Garrett said you'd be pissed. Did you *see*, Danil?" Her face was flushed, and a grin stretched across her young face.

Polly pursed her lips. "See what?" Clarke was too excited for this to be a usual encounter—though it was turning into a bit of a joke, now that Danil had missed every single one of them.

"It was a new kind of creature!"

Glad to be able to break the news to Polly, who couldn't spoil the fun by reading her mind, Clarke launched into a garbled description of the strange monster that had entered through the rift.

"But I didn't see its face because a remnant bashed its head in!" she finished. "And that's when Garrett told me I was the runner, so I bolted. I've already told Lord Francis and Master Julianne."

"Wait." Danil's face quickly passed from surprise to joy. "Julianne's here?"

Polly watched as indecision warred inside Danil. She knew how much he'd missed Julianne... But if Clarke's description was accurate, this creature was like nothing they'd ever seen before.

Would friendship win, or curiosity?

Danil's eyes met hers, and a grin spread over his face. "Come on," he said, and started sprinting down the trail, leaving her to grab their things and catch up with him.

She gathered their belongings together, shoving the cloaks at Clarke who took them with a hurried jerk of her head. Danil's lead was increasing.

Together, the two girls took off after him, jumping over a low farm gate as they gripped their bundles. As they reached the road, Danil hesitated for barely a second.

It was enough for Polly to catch up, but only for a moment. With a muttered, "Sorry, Jules," Danil took off again.

He headed not into town and towards the Mystic Master, but in the other direction. Polly stumbled, one foot already pointed towards Tahn. Clarke whooped in glee as she darted the other way, overtaking Polly.

Cursing, Polly snatched at a water skin that had started to slip and ran after them. Danil had pulled ahead again, but Polly had been trained by Tansy.

Keeping her elbows tucked and back straight, Polly focused on her legs, pumping them harder while keeping her steps light. Blood flooded her limbs, lending them power as she gained on Clarke.

The young performer glanced back just in time to see Polly on her heels. Squealing, Clarke plunged ahead.

Polly kept pace, not letting herself get distracted by the younger girl's excitement. She landed each foot precisely and forced her lungs to suck air in and out at a steady pace.

She saw her chance. The witchpost was ahead and beyond that, the freshly cut, paved road to Bastian's new school.

Polly darted down the old path while Danil ran ahead. Through the trees, she saw him wobble and side-step. *The bastard was using my eyes, then,* she thought with a smirk.

Polly focused her eyes ahead, feeling the earth thud against the soles of her feet as she ran. Hopping between fat roots and lifting her feet higher so she didn't trip over low branches, she pushed forward.

Another glance showed Danil through the trees, right by her.

I can beat him, she told herself. Clarke had already overtaken the mystic. *And I can beat her, too.*

The second would be a hard task. The young girl was fast

—*really* fast. Polly let her lungs gasp in three short, fast breaths… then, she roared.

As the two paths merged, Polly surged forward. Her feet hit the solid stones just ahead of Danil. His cry of disappointment echoed behind her, but she ignored it.

She had a bigger target in mind.

Clarke flung a backwards glance and yelped when she caught sight of Polly. Too starved of breath to make any sound, Polly bared her teeth in a ferocious grin.

They burst into the large clearing, darting past shocked builders and leaping over sawn logs and piles of cut stone. Clarke raced around the left side of the growing structure. Polly took the right.

When two feet slapped the smaller path leading towards the rift, each one belonged to a different girl.

Clarke's grin had faded, replaced with a frown of determination.

Polly blinked, the effort of the sustained run making her eyes water.

A tower peeked over the trees—their destination. *One last corner,* Polly told her legs. *Then you can give out. Ok?*

Banishing all thought and letting her body take over, Polly ran. Her breath came in ragged gasps, and as she put one foot down, she felt her leg wobble.

"Gah!" Her hands, numb from exhaustion, trembled.

The strap of the waterskin slipped, wrapping around her foot. She stumbled as everything she carried was jerked from her hands and scattered onto the dirt.

Polly lurched forwards, the tangled foot unable to find purchase as she twisted and fell. Her knees slid in the soft mud, and dirt smeared her face as she landed and skidded along the ground.

Polly jerked her head up in time to see Clarke race past her. A few moments later, Danil jogged up and offered her his outstretched hand.

"A few steps earlier, and you'd have lost," he said, grinning. "Not that losing to Clarke would be something to be ashamed of. That girl runs like the Bitch herself!"

Polly looked around, then rolled over to examine the damage. Dirt streaked her knees, hands, and elbows. A quick touch to her face and hair revealed she had well and truly 'eaten dirt'.

Then, Danil words sank in. Polly glanced at Clarke, who stood, hands on knees, grinning widely as she tried to catch her breath.

They'd finished paving the path to the rift days ago. *They paved the path*, Polly thought. She glanced at where the road ended, stones coming to a stop by the tall tower loaded with flares in case of a dire emergency.

"I won?" she asked, still not quite believing it. She could see the smear in the dirt just past the road's end, where she'd fallen.

"Bitch's oath, you did," Clarke chuckled. "Jakob will never let me live this down! Beaten by a townie. The *shame!*" she wailed, lifting a dramatic hand to her forehead.

"I won!" Polly screeched. "Bitch's tits, that was amazing!"

Danil snorted. "You might have won the race, but you're not getting a trophy for those manners!"

"I'd rather be fast than polite," Polly shot back. "Manners won't save you from a remnant."

"Fair point," Danil said, still grinning.

Polly took his hand, and he pulled her to her feet, inspecting one of her hands. She hadn't even noticed the sting in her palm where she'd scraped off the skin.

He gently brushed away the dirt with a corner of his shirt. "You'll probably lose the hand," he said.

She slapped him and jerked it back. "I know you mountain-folk are soft," she said, "but I think I can live with a few scratches. Now, we didn't race all that way to stand about lollygagging."

Danil brightened as he remembered why they were there. "Garrett?" he hollered, making the two guards nearby jump.

One of them chuckled. "Sorry, Mystic. He's gone. Took the beast to town to show Francis."

"What!" Danil screeched. "Don't tell me I busted my ass for nothing!"

The guards exchanged a glance and burst out laughing.

Danil narrowed his eyes. "Alright. Where is the the little pig-fucker?"

"Ye can't trick a mystic, boys, I told ye that!" Garrett stomped out from behind the tower. "Took yer sweet-ass time ta get here, didn't ye?"

Danil snorted. "If you'd sent the runner to me first, maybe I'd have been quicker."

"Aye, but where's the fun in that?" Garrett motioned Danil over. "Come on, I have ta get this ugly little prick to town. Hope ye weren't expectin' a rest when ye got here!"

Bette shouldered through the doorway behind him. "Stop yappin', ye mouthy shit. I need ye ta give me a hand with this wee pest, so we can get him back in one piece. Well... Three pieces. Ye know what I mean."

Garrett and Bette disappeared into the bottom level of the tower and emerged again a moment later, a board hoisted between them.

Danil peered over Garrett's shoulder. The spindly beast he'd seen in Clarke's mind was carefully stretched out, tied at each end to secure it in place. One leg was missing and a chunk of its head was splayed open.

"That's... disgusting." Danil couldn't think of a better word to describe the carnage. "Where's the rest of it?"

"In a bag on the table. Can ye get it fer me?" Bette asked sweetly. "I don't have enough hands."

Wincing, Danil peeked inside the room. A copper bowl sat on

a table, with a cloth sack inside. He stepped further in, and his sight vanished.

"Bette, come back. I can't see!" He groped for the table.

"Erm. It's probably best that way." Bette sounded uncomfortable.

Danil ran his hands along the table and found the bowl. He lifted the bag—it wasn't heavy, so he tucked it under his arm. When he wrapped his hand around the bottom, though, something thick and sticky coated his fingers.

Danil froze, and quickly realized whatever the substance was, it was soaking his clothes, too.

"Bette?" he called, voice flat.

"Yes, Danil?" Bette asked, sweetly.

"What's in the bag?"

She coughed. "The missing bits, of course."

As Danil stepped back outside, every set of eyes he was borrowing looked his way. He saw himself, hair mussed up from the frantic run, face pale, and mouth drawn tight as he considered what else he could see.

A cloth bag nestled under his arm. The top was tightly knotted, the corners of the white linen dropping down, ends slowly turning red as they soaked up the liquid that dripped from the bottom of the bag.

Deep red ichor soaked the bottom half of the bag. It oozed through his fingers and spread across his shirt.

"Bits of what, Bette?" he asked, just as sweetly.

"Him." Bette jerked her head over her shoulder, towards the alien body.

Danil gritted his teeth and took in a slow breath. "I'll get you back for this," he said. "Just you wait."

Laughter exploding behind him, Danil adjusted his grip on the bag—no point dropping it now, the damage was done—and strode off towards Tahn.

CHAPTER EIGHT

Lord George disembarked from his carriage, greeting Francis with a slap on the shoulder. "Glad to see you again, Francis. Looks like Lordship suits you!"

"Thank you, sir," Francis said, a pink flush creeping up his neck.

"Patrick, get one of the men to see to the horses." George waved at Julianne distractedly. "Keep them out of trouble, this time, will you?"

Patrick nodded seriously and jogged off to organize the entourage.

"Interesting choice of troop leader," Marcus commented under his breath.

"Lord George!" Julianne said.

George beamed and grasped her arms, leaning in to kiss her on each cheek. "My dear girl! So good to see you back. I trust your journey through the Madlands was uneventful?"

"Nothing we couldn't handle," she said, gesturing towards Marcus.

Marcus stepped forwards and bowed, then clasped Lord George's hand.

"Good job, soldier. Glad to see you're both safe and well. Bastian told me about that mischief in your homeland—bit of a tussle with that Donna, eh?" George raised his eyebrows knowingly at Julianne.

She smiled softly. "I believe the New Dawn is *officially* defeated."

"Just in time to face this new dilemma, too." George slumped a little and sighed. "Just when I think I can ease into retirement softly, another disaster rears its head."

"Retirement?" Julianne took his arm and led him towards Francis's house. "You're too young to be thinking of that, surely!"

George shook his head. "You flatter me, girl. But Adeline is practically managing the city now, with Jakob by her side. Do you know, she's already rebuilt the trade industry and started exporting medicines from our local herbalists?"

Julianne wasn't surprised. Adeline had a good head for business and the steadiness to make an excellent leader.

Raised voices caught her attention. Julianne stopped, glancing over at the cluster of soldiers. Patrick was toe-to-toe with one of his men, a ragged looking soldier with long, ratty hair down to his shoulders and four days' worth of growth on his face.

"New guards?" she asked quietly. Her eyes shone white as she dove into Patrick's head.

George snorted. "Mercenaries. Patrick might have a checkered background, but damned if he can't fight. His experience with remnant has saved more than one traveler these past months."

"So, you gave him a squad of his own?" Marcus said skeptically.

"I did," George said. "Only recently, I might point out. My own general has had some troubles keeping the hired fighters in line. Patrick offered to have a go at it, and he seems to be doing well enough."

"It was a good decision," Julianne said, to Marcus's surprise.

"It was?" The Lord of Muir sounded almost as surprised as Marcus felt.

Julianne nodded. "You've given Patrick purpose—and you took his men in. They will fight to the death for you. That other man, though…" Julianne frowned. "Lord George, be careful. That sort of greed and lust for violence almost always ends badly."

Worry settled in Marcus's gut. His eyes ran over the contingent of guards, picking out the few he remembered from the bandit attack on Lord George's convoy. The men looked different, face paint and ragged outfits swapped for the Muir livery.

Those men looked proud to be there. The others? Marcus recognized the look of resentment darted towards Patrick.

"Jules, you want me to keep an eye on them?" Marcus asked quietly.

She shook her head. "I need you at this meeting," she said. "Patrick can handle any trouble that crops up."

George watched the exchange curiously but didn't say anything. He let Julianne guide him inside and soon, the meeting was underway.

George slapped his palms on the table. "It doesn't matter what comes through that damn rip in the sky. The men just aren't there! You saw the guards I brought into town—half of them would fight for a demon if it offered them enough money!"

"Without the guarantee of safe passage between towns, the traders simply won't come to Tahn," Francis said patiently. "We've managed to keep rumors of the rift to a minimum, but we can't hide the increase in remnant attacks."

George sat back and sighed. "Five. I can spare five men and no more."

"Eight." Francis rested his own hands on the table, palms down.

"If you must have eight, half will be from the mercenary group." George flared his hands, chin wobbling as he capitulated.

"Why don't you mix up the guards?" Julianne asked. "Pairing the less reliable ones with a more seasoned officer may temper their bad habits a little."

"Perhaps." George sat back, drumming his fingers on the table. "I've been keeping them separate, but I can see how your plan could work. It might show the newer men what real honor and integrity look like."

Julianne nodded. "And your men will be able to quash any bad behavior. I don't want you getting stabbed in your sleep," she admitted. "Or sold to a demon," she added with a grin.

George sighed in relief. "I'll organize the change as soon as I return to Muir. My townspeople aren't exactly thrilled at the sight of these ruffians. There have been rumors... Well..."

Julianne turned as something fluttered against her mind. "Someone's coming," she said.

Conversation halted as they waited. A moment later, the door swung open, and Clarke stumbled back in.

She jerked to a stop when she saw Lord George. "Oh! Err, sorry, my lords. Bette said—and Garrett... Um." Flustered, Clarke stuttered to a stop.

"They're coming here?" Julianne prompted.

Clarke nodded. "But... Well, Danil..." She pulled a series of strange faces, eyes wide, mouth grimacing, and head nodding at Julianne.

Stifling a chuckle, Julianne jumped into her head.

"*Oh.*" Julianne stood. "I'd best go meet them at the gate."

George moved to stand, but she quickly put a hand on his shoulder. "No, no. Stay here. I'm sure you have lots to discuss with Francis."

She held her breath, hoping he would take the hint. She didn't want to use compulsion on him, but if he saw Danil in the gruesome state he was in...

"Well, if you don't mind going alone…" George settled back into his seat with a grin. "My old bones would rather stay put, anyway."

Julianne grinned. She waved Marcus down. "No, you stay, too. I'll be back as soon as I can."

Danil's mental tirade reached Julianne long before she saw him.

I fucking hate rearick, Danil thought loudly. *Mountain-loving, swill-suckers. Goat-humping, bearded fuckers. As lovable as sand in your ass-crack. Or, no, like one of those spiked river-worms that swim up your piss-hole and stab you with their tails.*

Someone's in a good mood, Julianne sent softly.

A fast, irritable barrage of images and sensations flooded her mind. The stench of old, warm blood; a ruined shirt; fingers glued together by a crusted, sticky substance hit her with all the annoyance that Danil felt.

The torrent continued for several minutes. Julianne was tempted to block the mental sending, but knew it was Danil's way of letting off steam. She let the feelings wash through her, despite the discomfort.

Even knowing what he felt couldn't stifle the quick giggle that bubbled up when she saw him.

Caked in old blood, hair on end where he'd thoughtlessly swiped at it with his filthy hand, Danil looked like he'd come from a glorious battle, not a sweaty trip through empty fields.

"Fuck you," he muttered. "Here."

He threw the bag at Julianne, who deftly caught it by the knotted ends. She held it out at arm's length.

"Go and wash," she said.

A wolfish grin finally lit up his features. "You don't want a hug from your best friend?" he threatened, spreading his arms wide.

"I dare you," she said with a grin of her own.

Sighing, Danil wandered off towards the barracks.

"Make sure you don't leave that mess in the horse's trough!" she called.

"I'll leave it in Bette's sheets if she's not careful!" he called back.

Julianne grinned and carefully placed the bag on the ground. She could sense the rearick coming and peeked out the gate.

"I'd avoid the barracks for a bit, if I were you," Julianne cautioned as Bette and Garrett paraded through, still carrying the corpse like a wounded soldier.

"Thanks for the warnin'," Bette said happily. "I'll send Gus down ta clean up after 'im. Bastard owes me a favor, he does."

"Take that to Francis's," Julianne said. "Try not to drip the entrails on the floor, though?"

Polly trailed in last and stopped to whisper to Julianne before she went past. "How mad is he?" she asked.

Julianne shrugged. "About as mad as you'd expect."

Polly nodded slowly. "I'd best go speak to him, then. I don't think Lord George would appreciate losing his captain *and* his lieutenant before he gets here."

"He's already here," Julianne said. "Are you sure you can calm him down?"

Polly nodded. "Anyway, he likes old George. I don't think he'd want to scare him. And Bitch knows, he's in a scary-ass mood."

Julianne sighed in relief. "I'll wait here. I want to see him before we go in."

Polly trotted off, soon returning with a soggy, but mostly clean Danil. His hair dripped, and his shirt was balled up in his hands, but at least the blood was gone.

Julianne spread her arms.

"Are you sure you want a hug?" Danil asked dubiously. "I'm all wet."

"As if I care," Julianne said.

He folded himself into her arms and she squeezed, inhaling his familiar scent and allowing their minds to touch.

Surprisingly, whatever Polly did had worked. Danil was calmer and even content, and Julianne felt his joy at seeing her. Though a trace of irritability remained, his mood had improved immensely.

"Is Bette safe to go to bed tonight?" Julianne asked.

Danil snorted against her shoulder. "Far from it," he said.

Julianne angled her head towards Polly, who shrugged innocently.

Whatever you're planning, I don't want to know, Julianne sent to her friend.

Plausible deniability? I can work with that, Danil silently replied.

He let go, pulling back to stretch his arms out. "You saw the beetle they brought in?" he asked.

Julianne nodded. "I saw it, and I don't like it. Danil, if there's one thing bigger than a vark on the other side of that portal, there's likely more. And who knows what else…"

"Vark? You named them?" Danil mulled it over as Julianne nodded. "Fair enough. It suits them."

"It was Bastian's idea."

He draped an arm over Julianne's shoulder. "Well, it's lucky we've got three clever mystics to come up with a plan, then, isn't it?"

CHAPTER NINE

Julianne looked around the table, wondering if her plan would work. Even if it did, there was no guarantee of a helpful result.

Lord George blinked slowly, fatigue setting in. Once he'd received the message from Bastian asking him to meet with the Mystic Master, he'd assembled his traveling guards and journeyed through the night to be here.

Danil, now dressed and back to his usual jovial self, gazed at Polly. Polly, in turn, chewed her lip as she did her best to avoid looking over her shoulder at the bug-like body behind her.

Francis and Bastian chatted quietly about the progress of the school. Now that the building was underway and Arcadian nobles were coming to evaluate progress, Bastian had begun to feel the pressure.

Julianne glanced at Marcus, who gave her a small smile. He nodded for her to speak, seeing she had something on her mind.

"I have an idea," she said abruptly. "I don't know if it will work, but I think it's something we need to try."

Danil sat up quickly, sensing the excitement in her tone. "What are you up to?" he asked.

"Before I left the Heights, Artemis and I were playing with the amphorald devices. He had a theory—but I haven't had a chance to test it out. I left as soon as the rearick brought the new bracelets up." She took a breath, aware she was talking too quickly.

Bastian cocked an eyebrow. "You're talking about a new spell, aren't you?"

She nodded, and Danil sucked in a quick breath. She let him nudge her mind, but resisted letting him in. She wanted to make sure she had the explanation—and the warnings—right.

"We might be able to create a link, similar to the three-way shields Rogan used. If we do that with the communication devices, there might be a way to send a signal to someone who doesn't have one."

Danil rubbed his bracelet, wrist still stinging where the needle had pierced his skin. He'd worn it less than an hour, but the security it gave—letting him stay in touch with those he cared about no matter how distant—made him wonder if he could ever take it off.

"But everyone that matters has one now," he said. He'd already used his to reach Margit, Jonsen, and Amelia. "Except Zoe. Bastard knows if that girl will ever return to the heights, now she's had a taste of freedom."

Julianne felt his fondness for the young mystic. "She had quite the adventure in the Dark Forest with the druids, but she has returned home. Still, you're forgetting someone. Two someone's, actually, though you've only met one of them."

She watched Danil work through the clues. When he connected the dots, his eyes shot open. "You don't mean…"

Julianne nodded. "If anyone knows what's going on, it's Ezekiel. I don't think it's entirely coincidence that this rift developed right after he left on his great adventure."

"Ezekiel? You mean, Founder Ezekiel?" George asked, bewildered. "I thought he was like Queen Bethany Anne—a mythical god, not a man who goes on adventures."

Julianne settled back in her chair. "He's as real as you or me. A little older, though." She ignored Danil's bark of laughter. "He left Arcadia before I did the first time. He didn't tell me much about where he was going, but I saw enough to know it would change the world."

"You just forgot to mention that?" Marcus asked.

"There was nothing to tell," Julianne said. "He was so vague. I just know Hannah was involved somehow."

"And Hadley?" Danil asked.

Julianne rolled her eyes. "That boy wouldn't have stayed behind if I'd tied him to a tree. No, Hannah was the key to Ezekiel's success, whatever his mission was."

"If she's as strong as you say…" Danil trailed off.

"Stronger." Julianne bit her lip. "At least, she will be if she's listened to anything I told her. If she's kept up with her practice, it may be even easier to reach her than the Founder."

Francis coughed. "Excuse me for interrupting—but it sounds like you've got a lot to deal with that doesn't involve Lord George and myself. Do you mind if we leave you to it?"

Julianne reached out to clasp his hand. "I'm sorry I haven't been very clear, Francis, but it's a very long story. We'll fill you both in later, I promise."

Francis nodded, then gestured to Lord George. "Mary will have lunch on by now, if you'd like to join me?"

Polly watched them go but didn't move. She sat still and quiet, as if hoping no one would notice she was still in the room.

"Polly, I'll need you to stay alert. If Marcus gives you a signal, you'll need to detach Danil's bracelet."

"What?" Danil yelped. "It hurt like a kick to the balls to get on, now you want her to take it off me?"

"Only if something goes wrong," Julianne reassured him.

Polly nodded. "What's the signal?"

"I'll swear like a sailor and jump on Jules like a rodeo rider," Marcus said. "Will that be clear enough for you?"

Polly laughed nervously. "Sure. But... let's not let things go wrong?"

"We'll do our best." Julianne leaned over the table, reaching a hand out to the two other mystics.

Danil took one and Bastian grasped the other. When their own hands were linked, Julianne let her eyes mist over.

"Here goes nothing," she said, then muttered something under her breath.

CHAPTER TEN

Julianne extended her magic out to Danil and Bastian, but instead of reaching out to them directly, she channeled her power through the amphorald.

Even recognizing when her power was funneled through the device had taken training and practice. Artemis had teased her, insulted her proficiency until Julianne could deliberately focus on the device embedded into her skin.

Meanwhile, the entire Temple had buzzed with news of a new shield. Artemis's mind link had never been seen, and almost every mystic present tried to expand on the technique by combining it with other spells.

The only one that seemed to be effective was mind communication, and even that had only given a minor improvement.

Now, however, Julianne had three Mystics with amphorald devices and a target worthy of their attention. If she could push far enough, hard enough, she just might catch the attention of Ezekiel or Hannah, his student. Both had the capacity for immense power.

It was this power Julianne sought as she linked with Bastian and Danil. Using their presence as an anchor, she pushed out with her magic, stretching it across Irth and into the far reaches of places she had never been before.

Julianne reached until her mind wavered. She fought past the tightening of her temples, questing out farther than she'd ever reached.

Time stood still. The sounds around her—the gentle rustle of paper in a breeze, a chirping bird outside—melded into a high-pitched hum. The feel of cloth on her skin became a restrictive coating across every inch of her skin.

Julianne pushed harder, seeking a glimpse of the immense power Ezekiel held.

Far beyond the boundaries of Irth as she knew it, something latent hummed. It was a source of power, but not human. Still, Julianne pulled, forcing her mind to thin and reach farther.

Her energy drained and hope sank.

Ezekiel. The name tore from her mind unbidden.

Jules? Jules!

Not Ezekiel. A girl.

Zeke's kinda busy. What's up? Hannah's mental voice was bright and soothing, giving Julianne the strength to hold on just a little longer.

Monsters. A portal. A hole in the sky. Images, memories of thoughts taken from others and of the dead beast behind her leaked through the bond with agonizing slowness.

Part of Julianne was aware that her thoughts were beginning to scatter and fracture. Foreboding cloaked her, but she didn't let go. This would be their only chance to find out what these things were—Julianne would not be able to expend this much effort again.

You mean the Skrima? Hannah sent a flash of imagery. *Damn, these bastards are popping up everywhere.*

How... stop... Blackness began to crowd out Julianne's thoughts like a noose. She had to hold on... just a little longer.

A hand touched her shoulder, but she shook her head, trying not to divert her attention to Marcus's warning.

Julianne, hold on. Hannah's presence flared brighter, reaching towards Julianne. *You've gotta shut down the portal. Those little critters? They're nothing compared to what else is out there.*

A demon rose before Julianne, humanoid in form with great tusks protruding from its scalp. She cowered, arms over her head as it rose above and sliced down with a red, glowing blade.

Buzzing in Julianne's ears formed words in a voice she didn't recognize.

We call it the rift. It is through that hole that she has been sending her creatures. Their attacks serve many purposes, but I believe she has been testing us for weaknesses. Preparing for a larger invasion. I think she wants to take this planet for her own.

Jules? Jules, I'm losing yo—

Hannah's voice faded, and Julianne slipped into the abyss.

CHAPTER ELEVEN

Julianne's head ached. The room was dark—no, her eyes were closed. She cracked one open and promptly shut it again when light stabbed her brain, making it scream.

"She's moving," Marcus said above her. "Can't either of you do something?"

"Not if she's burnt herself out." Danil sounded worried, and Julianne tried to form the words to reassure him that she was ok.

"Nrgghh." That wasn't what she'd intended to say...

"Gods, will she be able to speak again?" Francis must have come in. If Julianne hadn't been in so much pain, she'd have rolled her eyes.

I'm fine, dammit. Oh. They can't hear me. I need to say it out loud.

Julianne stretched her eyebrows up in an effort to lift her eyelids. It worked, and this time she steeled herself against the light, angling her glance away from the window above her with an effort.

The window *above* her? She felt around with her hands and realized she was on the floor. Squinting, she grimaced at Marcus.

"Jules?" He leaned down, obscuring the glare.

"Wa—water?" She worked her mouth, trying to bring some moisture back into it and banish the hoarseness in her voice.

"You're lucky I don't tip a pig's trough over your damn head." Danil leaned over, coming into view as he spoke. "Do you have *any* idea how stupid that was? Of all the slug-brained, idiotic, goat livered things you could—"

"Should I assume that the danger is over?" Marcus asked dryly. "Because a minute ago you were promising you'd never curse her out again."

"Not *my* fault the leader of the entire mystic community has a steaming pile of cowshit for brains." Danil disappeared, his stomping feet sending prickles of pain through Julianne's head.

"Wa—" Bastian appeared and lifted a cup to her lips before she could finish her demand.

Julianne swallowed thirstily, then rolled her tongue around her mouth. "We're in danger," she said in a low voice.

"Will this danger strike within the next few minutes, child, or can we take a moment to reassure ourselves of your safety first?" Lord George took her hand, and Julianne nodded.

She lifted herself up on one elbow, and he quickly helped her up as Marcus diligently assisted. Once she was back in her chair, she looked around the gathered faces, wondering how to explain what she'd learned.

What she needed to say was terrifying. Lord George and Francis had led their people admirably, but how would they defend against demons? Bastian and Danil would be able to see what was coming, once she'd recovered a little—but would it help them cope?

Her eyes turned to Marcus. She had no doubt he would stand and fight whatever came their way, but even his sword had its limits.

"The portals," Julianne said after a moment. "They're from another world."

Francis sat down, hard. "From another world?" he asked, voice unsteady.

"Yes." Julianne leaned back to accept the cold washcloth Polly draped over her forehead. It wouldn't do much to help with the thumping headache, but at least it felt nice.

"And you thought I was an idiot for trying to mind-link with a vark, who, as it turns out, is an alien," Bastian muttered. "Look, Master. *I'm* expected to do stupid stuff like risk my life in an experiment. You're supposed to be smarter than that... no offense."

Irritation prickled at Julianne, probably because he was right. She'd done something dangerous, and probably stupid, but it had paid off with a warning they'd be stupid to ignore.

"I'd add my support to Bastian's comments, but I'm sure you know where I stand." Danil's face was dark and angry. "Dammit, Jules! Why didn't you pull back? We could feel you breaking apart!"

Julianne shrugged. "I was too close to give up. But... there's more." She'd only touched on what Hannah had shared with her. A shudder crept over her skin.

"More?" Lord George asked. "More than aliens from another world, appearing through portals? I'm beginning to think that your actions will change our world."

"Can this wait?" Marcus asked. "Francis, do you have somewhere Jules can lie down?"

"Shh." Julianne waved down Francis's answer. "There's more. More than little varks and overgrown insects."

"What do you mean?" Danil leaned closer, curiosity finally getting the better of him.

"I mean..." Julianne took a breath, wishing she had the energy to just show them instead of relying on words to convey the impossible. Casting an image spell now was about as possible as flying up to touch the clouds.

"Go on, my dear," George said softly.

"Hannah showed me what else is out there. Demons. Huge, angry demons that lay waste to cities. And a presence, something so evil I couldn't begin to understand what it was." Julianne swallowed to hold back the urge to scream. "We *have* to close that portal. We have to do it now. Before…"

"Before a demon comes through," Danil whispered. "Bitch's oath, Jules. Couldn't you have just found a nice little planet with friendly paper-munchers?"

Julianne summoned a wavering smile, and Danil grinned back.

"Well, then, let's close this damn thing." Bastian stood, hands on hips. "I don't suppose Hannah showed you how?"

Julianne carefully shook her head. "She just said we have to close the portals. No matter what."

He nodded, opened his mouth, then stopped. A moment later his eyes grew wide. "You said portals? Plural. More than one?"

Julianne blinked slowly, gathering the fractured memories of her desperate conversation with Hannah. "She said… they're popping up everywhere."

Marcus rested his hand on her arm. "That means she's encountered more than one herself," he said, looking around. "And knowing Hannah, that means she's shut down more than one. Probably by herself."

"If she can do it, so can we." Julianne sat a little straighter, feeling hope penetrate the fog in her mind. "There must be a way, or she wouldn't have suggested it."

"Well, then," Lord George said, some of the color returning to his face. "I suggest we go about finding a way to do so. In the meantime, let's not scare the people more than needed, eh?"

Francis nodded. "This must stay between us, at least for now."

Bastian glanced out the window. "I agree."

Julianne nodded her consent. Together, they would face what was to come, and they would beat it.

CHAPTER TWELVE

The next morning, Marcus left Julianne with strict instructions to rest as much as she could. She'd fought him, of course—but a meeting scheduled with Lord George should at least keep her out of trouble.

With a smile of his own, Marcus eased the door shut to Danil's house and strolled off down the street.

Despite the news Julianne had delivered, nothing in the town had changed. *Why would it?* Marcus wondered. *Just because I know there are whole other worlds out there—worlds with monsters and Skrima and demons—Tahn has no reason to change.*

The thought reassured him, that no matter what they faced, there would always be places worth protecting.

He met Garrett at the gate just as Bette was returning from an overnight shift at the portal. The two had been informed of Julianne's conversation with Hannah, but seemed to have taken it in stride.

"Good mornin', ye big lug," Bette called with a wave. "Don't let me lieutenant here get ye into any trouble up at the crack!"

"The crack?" Marcus asked with a sideways glance at Garrett.

"Aye," Garrett said mournfully. "She won't let me call it the vagina, so now it's the crack—shits out monsters like a rabbit in a field full of laxative carrots."

"Yer a dirty minded wee shit, aren't ye," Bette teased. "It's a crack in the air, no cheeks to be seen. Or hair, so we know it's not Garrett's crack at least."

Marcus shuddered. "Please, no visuals. I'd like to eat again one day."

"Oh, but can't ye just picture runnin' yer fingers through the silky soft locks?" Garrett asked innocently. "I've almost got the ones up close to me nuts long enough to braid."

Marcus made a gagging sound and Bette erupted into laughter. "I wish I could tell ye he's lyin', but he's not!"

"Bitch's tits, stop!" Marcus pleaded. "If you say another word, you'll have to explain to Julianne why I suddenly can't—"

"Get yer dick up?" Garrett hooted. "There's a herb for that!"

"I was going to say keep my food down," Marcus shot back. He rolled his eyes and waved at Bette. "See you when we get back!"

"Not if he shows ye his hairy ass—ye'll spend the rest of yer life blind as Danil is!" Bette walked off laughing so hard she was nearly doubled over.

"Come on, ye prick. Stop lustin' over me beautiful ass." Garrett hoisted his axe over one shoulder and strode off down the road.

Wiping tears away, Marcus jogged to catch up. "I needed that laugh today," he admitted. "Bitch's oath, anything to take my mind off what's on the other side of that... giant vagina?"

Garrett snorted. "Ye've never seen a thing like it, but that don't mean we can't blow the fucker up. I'm a rearick, remember. I've spent me whole *life* blowin' shit up." He rubbed his chin. "Not all of it on purpose, mind ye."

Buoyed by the rearick's confidence, Marcus felt the tightness in his chest ease. "So, how are things back here since we left?

Apart from the giant vagina-crack, the remnant incursion and those new soldiers George found."

"Ye mean the ones that are uglier than the wrong end of a dog?" Garrett asked, scowling. "Aye, fuckin' peachy."

"Woah, what did I step in?" Marcus asked, startled by Garrett's sudden change in demeanor.

"Those hired swords aren't worth the shit they flush down the latrine after bad chowder." Garrett spat on the road. "Bully boys that never finished on their mother's teats, if ye ask me."

"Bullies?" Marcus asked. "That doesn't seem like something George would stand for."

"He doesn't know." Garrett shook his head. "And we can't prove a damn thing. Seen a hint here and heard a rumor there, nothin' clear enough ta take ta the old man."

"Still," Marcus said, "Shouldn't someone say something?"

Garrett sucked air between his teeth. "Most likely. We were goin' to mention it to George this visit. If it comes to a head here, we've got the mystic to crawl in their heads and see who's a dick and who's a rotten dick."

"I'll keep an eye out," Marcus said. "Julianne has already offered some suggestions."

"Anything would be an improvement," Garrett agreed. "As long as Bette don't kill one of 'em before we get the chance ta see yer lass's plans through."

"Ah." Marcus grimaced. "I see."

If Bette saw the new guards display anything but their best behavior in the town she was charged with protecting… it might be the guards who needed to be kept safe.

The walk to the portal was brisk, and Marcus had sweat running down his back by the time they got there. He rested one hand against the watchtower, letting the breeze cool his face.

"What, a few months on a mountain made ye soft?" Garrett scoffed.

Marcus straightened. "Soft? No. It's just a warm day."

"Aye, I find meself pinin' for the cold winds and black toes of the Heights on days like this one," Garrett said.

Marcus hesitated. "Black toes? Not exactly what I was missing, you strange little man."

"I'm no' little!" Garrett snapped, then stomped away.

"Where's this big vagina?" Marcus called after him.

Garrett flung an arm up, gesturing Marcus to follow him. Groaning as he left the cool shade, he did so.

Garrett pushed through some foliage, and Marcus trailed behind. When he got to the clearing just a few feet into the heavy undergrowth, he froze. "What the fuck?"

He blinked, but the razor-sharp slice taken out of the sky still hung there.

Garrett laughed. "Aye. That's what we all said the first time we saw it. Except Mack. I swear on the Bitch's own boots he said, 'want to fuck', not 'what the fuck'. Mack always did have strange taste in the lasses, though."

"Fuck you, tiny man." Mack waved cheerily at Marcus and headed over. "Watch the hole, Carey!" he called over his shoulder.

"Watch your own hole," Carey yelled back, but readied his spear and stood straighter anyway.

"Bitch's oath, Garrett," Marcus said, still staring at the rift. "If you think that's a vagina, I'd hate to see what you've been fucking in your spare time."

Mack let out a whoop of laughter as Garrett grumbled under his breath.

"How does anything fit through there?" Marcus asked. He walked closer, tipping his head to view the rift from different angles. No matter how he looked at it, the opening was paper-thin, and vanished as he tried to view it from the side.

"It stretches and heaves like a lass givin' birth," Garrett explained. "But don't let Bette know I told ye that. She thinks it's not polite or some shit."

Marcus stepped back. His mind raced, trying to make sense of the impossible passage between worlds. Then, he stepped forwards and lazily swung his arm around, slicing through it with his sword.

The sword slowed and caught, like a stick trying to cut through quicksand. Unseen forces grabbed at the blade, drawing it in.

Marcus's heart raced, and he yanked it back. The sword released with a low 'pop' that was felt, rather than heard.

"Watch this," Carey said. Without taking his eyes off the rift, he dropped into a squat. One hand felt along the ground until he found a rock. He stood, pointed his spear at the crack to aim, then pelted the stone.

It flew straight at the portal, which slipped and contorted around the rock. Marcus felt his stomach roil as he walked around. Half of the rock had just… vanished. Gone. Viewed from the right angle, the rock was invisible entirely.

The portal shuddered, then the rock dropped out with a soggy thud.

Marcus walked over, leaning as far away from the rift as he could, and kicked the stone closer to the watching men. It was coated in a shimmering red goo.

They watched as the substance evaporated, leaving a simple, unmarked stone on the ground.

"That was some creepy-ass shit," Marcus breathed.

"Aye! Fun, isn't it?" Garrett chuckled.

"Fun?" Marcus murmured, wondering what the hell Craigston was hiding if this was how rearick had 'fun'.

Garrett sighed. "Yer a bore." He turned to Carey and Mack. "You lasses can have a wee break. Us men have grown up things to discuss."

Mack snorted. "In other words, piss off, boys, we're comparing stories about our big vaginas."

Carey chuckled and lowered his spear. "Don't slack off. Bette will have our asses if she finds out we left our positions."

"Go fuck yerselves," Garrett said jovially. Once they were alone, he turned to Marcus.

"What the fuck are we goin' to do about this wee thing, eh?" He kicked at the rock and it flung upwards, lodging back into the edge of the rift. A few moments later, it fell back out.

Marcus approached carefully, one hand raised flat towards the opening. He waved it closer, only a hair's breadth from touching it. "It pushes the rock out, but it's not repelling my hand. Does it move at all?"

"Hasn't since we've been here." Garrett leaned close, squinting through the narrow gap with one eye. "What are ye thinkin'?"

"Maybe… we could build a wall. Some kind of barrier to stop anything getting through this end." Marcus watched the rock until it was clean, then picked it up again. "Has anyone stuck a hand in?"

"Do ye think we're fuckin' stupid?" Garrett squeaked. "Stick a hand it that? I'd rather shove me arm up a remnant's pussy."

"Don't involve me in your weird fantasies," Marcus replied. "What if we hold the rock in. Will it shove its way out, or stay there?"

"I don't fuckin' know." Garrett shrugged quizzically. "Why are ye so damn interested?"

"If one of those giant Skrima come through, we want to know how much force it would have to withstand. Or, if we bring down a mountain on it and some debris falls in, we need to make sure the whole thing doesn't end up unstable if the portal is shoving stuff back out." Marcus waited for Garrett to work through his explanation

Garrett watched as Marcus lifted the rock and pressed it against the portal. The edges shimmered and warped, wrapping around the stone and absorbing it in. Marcus held his hand up, just far enough away to avoid touching the rift itself.

He waited. The rock pressed gently against his hand but stayed mostly inside the rift.

"See?" Marcus said. "Now we know we can—"

The rift warped and shifted, spreading and stretching. The rock tumbled out below Marcus's hand and he jumped back, startled.

"Shit! I thought I was gonna—" Marcus scrambled back further as a spindly appendage slithered out of the rift. "What the fuck is that!"

The stick-like limb was spiked and folded down at the top. The rest of the leg soon followed, along with two bulging eye protrusions and a limp, dangling snout.

The creature—a Skrima, if Marcus understood correctly—tumbled out and landed on the dirt, dazed. It stood on wobbling legs, eye stalks moving independently of one another.

Marcus shuffled back, drawing his sword.

"Don't be scared, lad," Garrett chuckled. "They've never attacked anyone before."

One eye stalk turned towards Garrett. Then, the Skrima attacked.

It jumped, the deeply folded knees launching it in a blur of speed. Garrett screamed, and Marcus yelled for help, hoping Carey and Mack hadn't gone far.

He stabbed with his sword, but it glanced off the hard cara-pace on the creature's back. Scissor-like front limbs clawed at Garrett's neck, and a third pair pinned his wrists to the ground.

"I wasn't scared, rearick," Marcus grunted, slicing at a leg. The shell cracked, oozing deep red ichor, but the creature held on. "I was just being cautious."

"Cautious me the fuck out of here, then," Garrett called, voice strangled.

Another sword-swipe dismembered an eye-stalk, and finally, the creature reacted. It launched for Marcus, but he was ready for the speedy attack. He crossed both arms over his chest, gripping his sword tightly.

The Skrima tore at his forearms, trying to bury into his chest, but he held tight. The small front legs stabbed at his face, only to be fended off by the sword in its way.

"The eyes!" Marcus yelled. "Go for the eyes!"

An axe swung straight for Marcus's face, and he closed his eyes, hoping Julianne would shed at least a few tears at his funeral—if there was enough of him left to bury.

A wet thud exploded ichor and fluid all over his face. The spiked limbs stopped their urgent rending of his skin, though barbs still clung to his flesh. Marcus coughed and spat, nostrils filled with gunk.

He rolled, heaving and vomiting the remains of the busted Skrima's face onto the dirt.

"Ha! HA!" Garrett danced, waving his axe around. "I told 'em! I fuckin' told 'em all the little pricks were bad news! I was right!"

"You told *me* they wouldn't attack, you limp-dicked, shit-spewing little prick." Marcus gagged again and spat, trying to remove the acrid taste from his mouth.

"I'm not the one heavin' his guts up on the dirt," Garrett said sagely. He rested the head of his axe on the ground and folded his arms, leaning on it.

"Fair point," Marcus gasped. "Next time, I'll make sure it's you."

Garrett snorted, then helped Marcus to his feet. The rearick spun around. "Picked yer skirts up off the floor, yet, boys?" he bellowed.

Marcus looked over his shoulder and saw Mack and Carey standing, jaws slack. "How long have they been there?" Marcus asked.

"Long enough to have saved ye a face full o' alien squirt," Garrett snapped.

"Aliens? You know something we don't?" Mack said immediately.

"I know enough to know yer as useful as a couple of tits on a bull, ye wee shite." Garrett tossed his axe at Mack. "Clean me blade, and make sure ye get all the guts off. And make sure ye scrub Marcus's yak off the handle!" he yelled after Mack as he walked away, gingerly holding the ichor-soaked axe between two fingers.

"Sorry, boss," Carey said. "We were just so shocked... they've never attacked before."

"And how many do ye personally know, ye gobshite?" Garrett asked.

Carey blushed. "We've seen one of those before. It didn't hurt anyone!"

"It didn't have time!" Garrett yelled. "That remnant was on its ass like a boil before the stupid thing had time to move!"

Carey thought about that for a moment, then nodded. "You want me to send a runner to Tahn?"

"Ye'd best," Garrett said. "Who've we got?"

"Durrey, sir."

"Send 'im here before 'e goes." Garrett flicked a bit of cracked shell off his pant leg. "Ye need a bath, lad," he said to Marcus.

Marcus swiped at him in response but followed Mack back to the watchtower. Behind the makeshift building, he scrubbed the worst of the muck off in a horse trough filled with clean water.

Mack saw him gingerly lift his ruined shirt between two fingers.

"You'll want to burn that," Mack cheerily pointed out. "That shit stinks now, but give it a day and you'll think you've been fucking a month-dead remnant."

Marcus balled up the ruined shirt and tossed it at Mack. "Thanks for volunteering to clean it for me, buddy."

He ducked away before Mack could return the favor.

Across the clearing, Garrett was talking to Durrey in a hushed voice. "Direct to the Master, ye hear? Not a word past yer lips until yer in a room with her, and Bette if ye can find her."

"Yessir!" Durrey flashed a quick smile and snapped a salute

before taking off, bare heels kicking up dust as he sprinted towards Tahn.

"Are you sure it's safe to be sending kids running all the way back there alone?" Marcus asked. The question had bugged him since Clarke had arrived bearing her message the day before.

"I've seen 'em run past a damn pack, and leave 'em wonderin' who kicked up the dust," Garrett said. "And it's better than havin' 'em skulkin' 'round in the trees, hopin' for a look. At least if they're bein' useful, we know where they are."

"I suppose," Marcus said. "Still. Seems dangerous."

Garrett nodded, chewing on his moustache. "I don't like it any more than yerself, lad. But we need fast legs, and the horses won't stay more'n a few minutes."

"Speaking of terrified beasts," Marcus said. "Where's the local remnant brigade? I came out thinking they were lurking in the forest, just waiting to pounce on the next Skrima that tumbled through your big vagina."

Garrett shrugged. "They sometimes come, sometimes not. If they're around, though, they rip the wee red bastards to shreds, with no regard for their own selves."

"That's pretty typical for a remnant, though." Marcus pulled his boots back on.

"Not like this, lad. They're crazed, out for the total destruction of the beasts. Not for fun or food, or even the hunt. It's... different." Garrett rubbed his face, then rolled his shoulders to loosen them.

"Crazy," was all Marcus could say.

Garrett shrugged. "At least the little prick was easy to kill."

Marcus nodded. "One was. I don't like to think about what we'd do facing an army of them."

Garrett spat. "Now yer just askin' for trouble!"

Marcus laughed. "You wouldn't want it any other way."

Garrett raised his fist to bump against Marcus's. "Aye, lad. Ye've got that right!"

CHAPTER THIRTEEN

Bette knocked on the door, nerves making her effort weak. She cleared her throat, straightened, and knocked again. This time, the sound was strong and clear.

"Come in, Bette." Julianne's voice was muffled through the thick door.

Bah, so much for a good impression, Bette thought. The mystic would have sensed her there... and noticed her fluttering anxiety. Still, Julianne had let her knock the second time. Bette could still make a good impression on Lord George.

Though she'd spoken to him many times, it was almost always in battle. Or just before it. There had also been a few times when she had been covered in the blood and gore of slain enemies. That was when Bette was in her element.

This scheduled meeting had been planned days ago, though, and had the feel of something more formal than her casual discussions with her superior.

Pull yer knickers up, lass, she told herself. *Ye always get yerself in a knot when it comes ta talkin' to the big boss—and ye always come out on top.*

Bette pushed the door open, a nervous grin plastered to her face. She walked over to the table, ignoring Julianne and Bastian. She spared the platter on the table loaded with fruit, bread, and ham an admiring glance.

Bette gave Francis a polite duck of the head and dropped an awkward curtsy to Lord George.

"Good mornin', me lord."

Pleased that she'd pulled off the complicated maneuver, she dropped into the nearest seat. Curtsies were ridiculous at the best of times, but she was wearing her best pants. Last time she'd worn them, they'd been loose, but in her time as captain, the muscle she'd built made them tight across her backside.

"Good to see you, Captain Bette," George said with a kind smile. "No need for formality, though. I've always enjoyed your honest approach."

Relaxing a little, Bette reached over the table and grabbed a handful of plums from the bowl. "What've I missed?"

"Not much," Francis admitted. "We're at a loss. You were filled in about the source of our new friends?"

"Aliens from another world?" Bette snorted. "Aye. I don't see what it matters, though. They're pests, and the portal is a security issue. Both need to be dealt with."

"Pests?" Julianne asked. "They're not that bad." To prove her point, she sat Ardie on the table, patting his back until he unfurled and stretched out on his belly.

"You have one tamed?" George asked, face lighting up. "Oh, do say I can give him a pat!"

Julianne nodded, and Bette watched the old man reach out to gingerly touch the alien creature. Like a child with a kitten, he grinned and picked it up, cuddling it to his chest.

Bette shook her head, but couldn't help the tiny smile that touched her lips. "Oh, fine. They're a wee bit cute."

Francis didn't look appeased. "The varks seem benign, but what about your vision, Julianne?"

Sobering, Julianne nodded.

"Ye'll have to explain that one to me," Bette piped up. "Giant demons? Through that wee hole? Even the tiny beasties like yer pet there have trouble shovin' their way through the split."

Julianne closed her eyes, brow wrinkling as she recalled the snatches of information Hannah had sent. "The rifts can grow and get stronger. Ours was much smaller than the one Hannah showed me."

Bette didn't question how Julianne had compared the two. As far as she was concerned, the mystic's power was absolute—and the less Bette knew about it, the better.

Battle magic was one thing. Bette had even come to terms with the need for healing magic. But the events at Tahn had solidified her natural aversion to magic. All other forms of magic could just stay the hell away from her, thank you very much.

"It's no' just the varks or the big spooky demon-lad ye think may come for us," Bette said. "Somethin' has the remnants in a dither, and they're making a goat-cocked nuisance of themselves around town."

George let out a loud, undignified snort. "Goat-cocked," he murmured. "Must keep that one in mind."

Julianne hid a smile, but Bette grinned widely. The old Lord had a love of vulgar curses, though she'd never heard him use one himself.

"Bette's right," Francis added. He shrugged. "Seems like no matter what happens, we're screwed."

"How bad is it?" Julianne asked. "I mean, I've seen the reports, but that doesn't tell the whole story, does it?"

Francis shook his head. "It's not just sightings. We've got people coming across what look like temporary camps, and we've had livestock disappear. It's been a really rough winter."

Bette rested her palms on the table. "I've been doin' what I can, and so have me soldiers. Night patrols only go so far, though, and with takin' away me best fighters to watch that ass crack shittin' out wee rock creatures, we're stretched thin."

"I did offer to send some of my army," George said.

"Aye, ye did." Bette's expression darkened, her thick eyebrows lowering into a glower. "But ye either have to send me yer dregs or send decent men and leave those rough-headed shit-munchers in yer city."

George sat up at that. "What are you talking about?"

Bette's face flushed bright red. "I apologize, me lord. That wasn't right for me to say, not when there's no proof of anything what may have happened."

"Proof of *what?*" George asked, bewildered.

Bette groaned. "Ach. I'm so shite at this diplomacy rubbish!"

George clicked his tongue. "Well, then diplomacy can go and… lick a…" he racked his brain for a moment. "Can go lick a sandy dog turd!" George grinned and looked around the table, beaming in pride.

Bette erupted into laughter. "Ye did good, there, me lord. Fair enough, I'll tell it to ye straight."

"Please, do," Francis said, voice tight. His eyes brimmed with tears as he did his best to hold back giggles.

"The House of Friendship went and put out a notice, sayin' those new fighters ye hired are banned. We heard from a trader— he wouldn't say nothin', except that it was past time, but he hoped those traveling' the roads wouldn't suffer for it."

George digested the information slowly. "But why were they banned? And why would the traders feel any repercussions?"

Bette nodded knowingly. "That's what he wouldn't say, me lord. Shut right up, he did, when we tried to ask. And so did anyone else who happened to catch themselves facin' the same questions."

George's expression closed in, his face smoothing over into something bland, yet somehow very dangerous. "What else?"

Bette shrugged. "Nothin' else. That's just it. Not a damn word since. We knew ye were comin' here, so we wanted to talk to ye direct—we didn't expect the bastards to come with ye!"

"Of course, if no one will come forward it will be very hard to prosecute. We're not even sure what the charges are," Francis said. "Unless…" His eyes slid to Julianne.

The mystic looked as relaxed as Lord George—or like a viper ready to strike. "Unless someone had the magical ability to find out what's going on from the men themselves."

George jerked his head in a rough nod. "I know your people tend to avoid intruding on people's minds uninvited—"

"Oh, no," Julianne cut him off with a wicked grin. "That only applies to people we like."

George smiled, but his face stayed cold. "Well, then. As soon as we finish here, I'd like to formally request you interrogate my men and find out what they've done to deserve such a reputation."

Julianne nodded. "That doesn't help our immediate issue, though. If you like, I can contact Amelia—she's the Chancellor of Arcadia. I've mentioned her before?"

George nodded, but Bette grimaced. "You don't think we should call on her aid, Bette?" he asked.

Bette bit her lip. "I just don't like the idea of relyin' on someone way across the Madlands ta be runnin' to our rescue every time we catch a problem." Her eyes met Julianne's. "And besides, doesn't the lass have her hands full as it is?"

"She's busy, and short-handed," Julianne admitted. "But she wouldn't have offered if she couldn't spare some assistance."

"Aye, and if a city that was half-burned to the ground barely a year ago can send help, what's wrong with our own selves if we need it?" Bette asked.

George gave a brisk grunt. "I feel the same, my girl. We've enough people in our lands—they may not be fighters, but they'll need to be just that, if they want to protect their own lands."

"What about the outlying communities?" Julianne asked. "I

know that Patrick came from one of them. Do you think we could send to them for assistance?"

"You'll more likely be asked to provide it," Francis said warily. "If we didn't have the might of Muir behind us, and the help and training Bette's given, we'd be begging for soldiers to offer protection. That's if we'd survived this long."

"Bah, ye built a damn wall heavy enough to keep out the worst of them," Bette said. "And ye did that yerself."

Francis allowed himself a small grin at that. "Still, if there are small towns without a proper garrison, we may end up stretching ourselves thinner."

"If that's what happens, that's what we'll do," Bette said. Realizing she may have overstepped, she looked to George. "With yer permission, me lord? I don't think ye'd be the sort to leave whole towns at the mercy of those rot-faced shit-eaters."

"Whatever it takes, Bette. We must keep our people safe!" George thumped his fist on the table. "If they aren't under my protection, and they don't have anyone else's, we can't let them suffer. Do what you must, but we *will* make the region safe."

Bette grinned, her adoration for their lord increasing. "Aye, me lord. If the small towns pull up as well as Tahn, they won't need much but some trainin' and a few lessons on weapon-smithin'."

George sighed. "I do hope we don't bite off more than we can chew, but I can't leave innocent people as remnant fodder. Still, if we can find a way to close the—"

Shouting in the street cut Lord George short. As one, the people in the room shot to their feet. Bette yanked her sword from her belt and ran for the door, then paused. "Julianne?"

The mystic's eyes were already white. "Go!" she urged Bette.

Bette burst out of the door to find a crowd of people milling about. She shoved past two men, then pushed a woman out of the way to see Sharne, one hand around a soldier's throat.

"And next time, I'll slit your throat instead. Hear me?"

The soldier smirked. "Like to see you try it, love. Think your little farmboy soldiers can take on all of us at once?"

Sharne stepped back, letting the man free. "You think we can't fight." It wasn't a question, but a statement delivered in a flat voice.

The soldier laughed, and a smatter of chuckles in the crowd made Bette notice who was watching. Most of those present were Lord George's hired hands.

Julianne watched as the men shuffled. She recognized those who were Patrick's men—they moved back, hands on weapons as they eyed their fellow guardsmen with outright suspicion.

One in particular caught her eye. Thumbs through his belt loops, he looked on with a smirk, a glint of fire in his eyes. It was Patrick—and he *wanted* this fight to break out.

"Fight? I'm not gonna to fight you, love. I'm gonna fuck you!"

Bette surged past the edges of the crowd, reaching Sharne a moment too late. The wet smack of a fist in a jaw rang out through the shocked silence at the soldier's words.

The peace broke in a wave. The crack of fists was echoed by cries of support from the crowd, some in favor of Sharne and others egging on the man who had her in a headlock.

The soldier dropped Sharne to the ground and straddled her.

Bette felt the blood drain from her face. *Ohhhh, shit on a stick.* This wasn't going to end well.

The soldier ground his hips on Sharne, who lay still. She looked up, eyes wide.

"Like that, bitch? A good fuck will loosen you up, you tight-snatched whore."

It was all Sharne could take. She bared her teeth in a ferocious grin. Then, in a blur of movement, flipped her attacker over so that he was flat on his back, Sharne kneeling over him, spear in hand.

"You need a dick to rape a girl, love." She ground her knee into his groin, pressing harder when he squealed in agony.

Bette sighed. "I *knew* it'd end bad."

She watched as Sharne lazily grabbed the arm of a man who tried to pull her off. A moment later, he was on the ground next to his friend, though this one had the sense to cross his legs.

Sharne kicked him in the head, buying her enough time to deal with the third man. She parried his sword strike with her spear, tripped him, and stabbed his thigh. "You're lucky that wasn't your cock," she spat.

When two more soldiers made to join the fray, Bette stepped in. Sharne faced off against the man she'd head-stomped, while Bette stood at her back, sword raised.

The crowd exploded. Townspeople screamed and ran, while others did their best to fight off armed soldiers with fists and baskets. A small handful of soldiers turned on their own as Patrick's men launched into the fray, protecting the citizens.

Bette rammed her sword into the gut of a leather-clad fighter, grimacing at the waste of a life.

She slapped her pommel at someone's temple, and grinned as he crumpled to the ground. Two men came barreling at her, and she ducked and rolled, coming face to face with Patrick.

"Bout time someone showed that pig-fucker some manners," he grunted, then lunged towards Bette, sword out.

She yelped and threw herself to the ground. Blood squirted on her arm, and she darted a look up to see Patrick sliding his sword from the chest of one of his own men.

"What the fuck are ye doing?" she yelled. "I'm in me good pants! Don't bleed 'em on me!"

Patrick laughed and nodded. "Fair enough."

He spun and ran, dragging away a soldier flicking his fist. Jessop was reeling away from him, cheekbone split.

Bette growled but turned away, satisfied the offender would

be dealt with. She caught sight of Mary, the tavern-owner. The wrinkled woman thrust a metal baking tray up as a blow glanced off it, then shoved the hard edge forward.

The soldier who'd attacked her was caught off guard. When Bette attacked, he was less surprised—but only because he was dead before he'd realized she was there.

Bette jerked her head around. The remaining soldiers stood, hands in the air, faces terrified.

"I can't move!" one whimpered. "I can't move! Something's got my body!"

Julianne stepped outside, eyes white, knuckles tight on her staff. She gestured while murmuring something. The seven men walked to Francis, who calmly held out several lengths of rope. Silently, the soldiers began tying each other up.

"Oy!" Bette yelled. "Not that one!" She pointed at Patrick, who suddenly dropped his rope, shook himself, and scrambled away.

His eyes darted around.

"Oh, grow some balls, ye pussy. It's what ye get for ruinin' me clean shirt." Bette held his gaze until she was sure the panic had eased, then turned to Julianne.

"I see," the mystic said. Two more men were released from her psychic prison. "Bette, I'm still a little tired from yesterday. Could you address the ones who are injured?"

"Address them how?" Bette asked, hopefully.

"Non-lethally," Julianne said.

Bette's face fell, but she snatched up one of the dropped ropes and walked over to a groaning soldier on the ground.

Her eagerness returned when she realized it was the man who'd started the fight with Sharne.

"And what did ye do to me troop leader, ye scum-shitting crap-licker?" she asked as she bound his wrists to his ankles.

"Frigid slut," he grunted through his broken mouth.

"Now that doesn't even make sense," Bette said. She left him with a swift kick to the skull, shrugging when Julianne caught her eye. "What? I tripped!"

Julianne snorted, but didn't say anything.

"Now," Bette said, resting fists on her hips. "Are ye goin' ta tell me what the fuck just happened, and why me good pants are all caked in goat-fucker?"

CHAPTER FOURTEEN

Sharne rested the steak gingerly on her face, reclining on a bed behind Francis's office. "I feel like such an idiot."

"Sounds like the bastard deserved what he got," Bette said.

"I don't regret that. I just can't believe I let one of the pricks knock me out cold!"

Sharne had explained why the fight started. She'd been going to start her shift, when she had come across one of the soldiers hassling a young village girl. When Sharne had caught his attention, he'd simply walked up and grabbed her ass, pulling her close and trying to kiss her.

Thoroughly revolted, Sharne had shoved him off and given him a lecture, then told the entire troop to get the fuck out of Tahn.

They'd thought that was hilarious.

The fight broke out, and Sharne had eventually been taken down by a punch to the jaw.

"And what's yer story, then?" Bette darted a glance to Patrick, who'd shamefacedly brought the meat and tried to slink away.

Patrick sighed. "I knew they were dicks. Plenty of rumors—

always are about men like us, but this was different. Not stories spread in bars, but whispers in the street. I couldn't get anyone to actually drop a name, though."

"Too scared?" Bette asked.

He nodded. "I tried to offer protection, but fear won out."

"So ye thought ye'd let us clean up yer mess?" Bette's disgust was clear in her voice. "Ye thought ye'd risk *my* soldiers?"

"Risk?" Patrick laughed. "I've seen them fight, Captain. There was no risk... uhh, of death, anyway." He turned to Sharne. "Sorry about your face, though."

Sharne groaned. "It was worth it."

Patrick raised his hands. "See? I knew your lot would kick their asses. And really, I don't think I could have stopped that fight breaking out even if I'd wanted to."

Bette narrowed her eyes, unhappy that she might just have to agree with his logic.

A shadow filled the doorway, and Lord George lumbered in. "Next time, my boy, take your concerns to someone who can deal with them, eh?"

Patrick nodded. "I owe you an apology for that, Lord George. I didn't want to catch you between rumor and hearsay, but I guess keeping quiet didn't make things any better."

"That's right. If I'd known, I'd have sent for a mystic and cleared it up right away." Lord George rested a hand on Patrick's shoulder. "Thank you for stepping up when it counted, though. I saw you fighting."

"Ye call that fightin'?" Bette scoffed. "Ye need a week in the trenches with Sharne, here. She'll have ye fightin' like a real man."

Patrick laughed nervously. "Maybe."

"Fantastic idea." Lord George looked around, beaming. "Sharne, if you return to Muir with me and train up some of our aspiring soldiers, it may fill some of the gaps." George pursed his lips.

The 'gaps' had just increased. Bastian had taken on the task of interrogating the offenders, but it was unlikely any would find a place back in the guard again.

"We can deal with the numbers later," Bette said. "Got plenty to keep us busy in the meantime."

"Yes." Lord George sighed. "We do need to finish our meeting, and I believe Sharne here needs to rest. Shall we retreat?"

Bette lingered for a brief moment once the men had left.

"Sorry, Captain." Sharne winced at the pain of speaking.

Bette chuckled. "Ye did well, lass. How do ye feel about goin' to Muir?"

"Me? In the big city?" Sharne thought for a moment, then shrugged. "I guess, as long as it stops old George from having to hire on more dick wipes like those guys…"

"That's the spirit." Bette stepped outside and gently closed the door, hoping Sharne would have the sense to sleep.

"And there was no mention of how a portal might be closed?" Francis was saying as Bette took her seat.

"No," Julianne said with a sigh. Her head ached from the burst of magic she'd used, and she made a note to thank Danil and Bastian for taking over as soon as she'd called them. "We might have to count on our first attempts failing."

"Garrett loves ta play with things that go boom," Bette interjected. "He might have an idea or three. Of course, they might be really fuckin' terrible ideas…"

"It's Garrett," Julianne pointed out. "Of course, they're terrible ideas. But, it might be just what we need."

"Aye," Bette agreed. "But don't let *him* know that. His head's already big enough."

"If we can't blow it up, maybe we can wall it off?" Francis asked. "I've seen them come through—it looks difficult. If they were to encounter a solid barrier, maybe that would make it too hard to push through."

"A reasonable suggestion," Lord George said, looking to Julianne.

"That might work," Julianne said.

"And if it doesn't?" Francis asked. "We need a plan C. Any ideas?"

Julianne frowned as heads shook around the table. "Actually… I might. Or, not an idea as such." Her conversation with Bastian replayed in her head.

"Spit it out, lass," Bette said.

"I think the varks are sensitive to mind magic," Julianne said. "Remember how Bastian said they may even be susceptible to it?"

"What? Like a human?" Bette screeched. "Not a bat-slapping chance! A druid would have more chance at magicin' 'em, wouldn't they?"

Julianne shrugged. "Not necessarily. The creatures beyond the rift are somehow linked to our nanocytes."

Blank looks surrounded her. "The tiny things in our blood that give us magic are called nanocytes," she explained.

Bewildered nods didn't give her any more confidence.

"We'll take your word for it," Lord George said. "Though, I admit I don't understand it. Not at all. But, if you can take this information and formulate a plan, I won't argue."

"At this point, I don't know how it will help us, but I plan to investigate further," Julianne said. She fiddled with the tablecloth.

"Am I to assume we shouldn't discuss this plan with Marcus?" Francis asked carefully.

"What? Yer plan's half-cracked, ain't it?" Bette slapped her knee, laughing. "Bitch knows ye won't be able to keep 'im in the dark. That lad has a nose fer yer crazy ideas!"

"She's right," Julianne admitted. "I'll tell Marcus when he gets back. He won't be impressed, but we need to know more about the varks, and whatever else might be out there."

"We won't need to know more if we can stop them coming

altogether," Francis pointed out. "Why don't we try the safer plans first?"

"Ye think lettin' Garrett loose with a cask of powder and a match is *safe?*" Bette asked.

Francis sighed. "This isn't going to end well, is it?"

CHAPTER FIFTEEN

Danil led the surly rearick towards the tiny tavern. Mary was outside, lighting the lanterns as dusk settled.

"Evening, Mary," he called.

"Evening, Danil, Garrett." Mary hung the last lantern on its hook. "Dinner, or just drinking tonight?"

Garrett mumbled something under his breath, and Mary sighed. "I'll pour the drinks. Danil, don't you let him go crazy tonight, you hear?" She wagged a finger at the mystic.

Danil laughed. "I promise I won't, Mary. And despite my friends festering mood, we'll eat, too."

When Garrett protested, Danil shuffled him past. "You're mad as hell, and you need a few stiff drinks. If you don't eat, you'll end up puking in the bushes again. If Mack catches you, he won't let you live it down for weeks."

"It was three months since last time!" Garrett whined. "And he still brings it up every time I raise a mug to me lips. Soft-cocked cheese monkey."

Danil lifted an eyebrow in response to the half-hearted insult, and guided Garrett to a table in the corner. He hoped Mary's wouldn't be busy tonight.

"Look," he began. "I know you're angry, but—"

"Angry? The bastard made a pass at one of me guards! And grabbed her ass!" Garrett snarled. "I'm not angry, I'm fuckin' livid."

"Sharne ground his face in the dirt—and his nuts. She's fine!"

"Aye, but that's not the point, is it? And Patrick, the gall o' the bastard. Bringin' 'em here!" Garrett crossed his arms resolutely. "Ye won't change me mind about that one, I'm tellin' ye."

"His hands were tied," Danil said. "Come on, Garrett. If someone came up to you and said half your soldiers were lecherous bullies, but wouldn't say who it was, what would you do?"

"I'd drown the fuckin' lot of 'em," Garrett snapped.

"Here, maybe. What about back in the Heights?" Danil knew the rules and regulations in Garrett's hometown were a lot tighter than on this side of the Madlands, especially for a low-ranked guard.

Garrett pouted. "It's not the same."

"It's not that different, either." Danil raised a hand to accept a mug from Mary, forgetting to look up, though he grasped it perfectly.

She slapped his hand. "Just because you don't *need* to look at someone, doesn't mean you don't owe them the courtesy of doing so, young man."

Danil grinned sheepishly and turned to give her a look, letting his eyes clear for a moment even though it meant darkness fell over him. "Sorry, Mary."

"With eyes like that, it's no wonder that Polly is knee deep in love with you," Mary sighed.

"I know you can't resist my sparkle," Danil joked.

Mary slapped him gently again before disappearing back behind the bar.

"He should have done differently," Garrett said, refusing to let the matter go.

"Garrett, he didn't know who was causing the trouble. He

didn't even know for sure if they were!" Danil pushed Garrett's mug in front of him.

The rearick's nose twitched as bubbles drifted up to tickle it. "Gut feelin'. If he don't have it, he shouldn't be leadin' no one."

"You've got that because you were trained well and brought up through the ranks in a structured environment," Danil said patiently. "Patrick is a farmer who was abandoned by his lord. He's got trust issues, a guilt complex, and a really bad dose of insecurity in his new position."

Garrett lifted an eyebrow at that. Then, unable to resist, he snuck a sip of his drink. His eyes closed as he savored the thick mead.

"And I suppose ye've been searchin' through his head, then," Garrett said once the drink had slid down his throat.

Danil nodded. "The man is as twisted up as wool on a spindle, but he's trying, Garrett. You can't hold him to your standards."

Garrett sighed. "Fine. Ye prick. I'm only givin' in so ye stop yer yappin', by the way." He took another swallow of his drink. "Drink as good as this should be enjoyed in silence."

Danil sat back, pleased he'd convinced the rearick. He spotted Mary and hailed her over.

She waved back, but stopped at the door to greet Mack, Carey, and Lewis. When she came over, Danil asked what she was cooking for the evening meal.

"Brisket and roots tonight," she said promptly.

"I'll take a plate, please. I don't think Garrett is hungry, though." Danil bit his lip, trying to keep a straight face.

Garrett was still staring in Mack's direction, eyes smoldering. "What? I'll eat, damn ye. A big plate, thanks, Mary."

"Wise choice, my friend," Danil said with a snigger.

"Garrett!" Mack spotted the two men sitting in the shadowed corner. "Come to fertilize the bushes again?"

"Get fucked!" Garrett called back, before turning to Danil. "Can't ye make him forget that?"

Danil rubbed his chin. "It wouldn't be a very ethical use of my magic."

"Oh, and that trick ye did on Polly to make ye… *proportions* change was ethical?" Garrett waited expectantly.

Danil blushed. "How did you hear about that?"

"Polly told Bette." Garrett drummed his fingers on the table. "I haven't told a soul… *yet.*"

Danil opened his mouth, closed it, then sighed deeply. "You've got me over a barrel. Just… don't tell Jules. Of *either* thing."

"Aye, I'm sworn to secrecy!" Garrett said gleefully.

"And you owe me a favor. Deal?" Danil said.

"Yeah, yeah. Anything ye want!" Garrett gestured for him to get it over with.

"Hey, Mack!" Danil called. "Tell me about that time Garrett threw up in the street." He whispered something afterwards too low for Garrett to catch.

"Sure! We were drinking, and he… um… we were…" Mack faltered and scratched his head. "What were we talking about?"

Carey snorted. "I think Danil just bamboozled you. You were telling us your fortieth rendition of the night Garrett puked his guts out."

"Garrett puked?" Mack asked, bewildered. "Was he sick?"

"Ahh, fuck," Garrett muttered. "Ye giant smokin' asshole."

Hoots of laughter filled the tavern. Lewis slapped the table. "He made you forget! Ha!"

"Forget what?" Mack wore a worried expression.

"Garrett got piss drunk one night, oh, just before the winter started to break." Lewis rubbed tears of laughter from his eyes. "He went too hard, too fast. You caught him heaving his guts outside on Mary's rhododendrons. Every time you've seen him with a drink since, you've reminded him."

Garrett's face was a ruddy, angry red. He rose, chair sliding back noisily. "Ye prick! Ye set me up!"

"Hey!" Danil raised his hands defensively. "I did what I said! He forgot!"

"Oh, I forgot, alright," Mack yelled. "But I won't forget this!"

Garrett collapsed into his chair with a groan. "I suppose I fuckin' asked for that."

Danil couldn't hold his laugher in anymore. He held his sides, heaving for breath. "Never... *never* try to... blackmail a mystic," he wheezed. "Especially not a prick like me!"

Garrett downed the rest of his drink in one long swallow, then slammed it on the table. "MARY!"

Mary yelled out from the kitchen. "Hold your horses, meal's coming!"

"Bring me a Bitch-damned jug of that mead!" Garrett demanded.

A moment later, Mary stalked out juggling two plates and a pitcher of mead. She carefully set the plates down, then held out the jug.

"Hurry up, lass," Garrett said.

Mary smiled sweetly, then tipped the entire jug over his head. "By the way, there's a thirty-percent surcharge on jugs tonight, and an extra fee for bad manners."

Garrett opened and closed his mouth like a fish, too shocked to answer before she walked away.

Danil just stared, disbelieving, his view of the events skewed from watching through Garrett's eyes.

The room was quiet until Mack spoke up, his voice low but clear in the silence. "I don't remember Garrett heaving his guts up, but I'll wager this is a *much* better story anyway."

CHAPTER SIXTEEN

George climbed into his carriage and signaled he was ready to go. Julianne leaned down from her horse.

"You're sure you can make it from the portal road to Muir with six men?" she asked dubiously.

"One of these men is a woman," Lord George pointed out. "I think that tips the scales."

"I've been through the rest stop since it was fortified," Sharne said. "It's very secure, so we'll be safe to spend the night. The bulk of the remnant trouble is down our way, anyway."

Julianne nodded. "Let's move out, then."

They rode fast, stopping only when three remnant barred the road with hungry looks. Sharne slid off her horse and ran in with Patrick on her heels. The four men left in the guard quickly caught up, and the remnant were easily dispatched.

When they resumed travel, Julianne lightly brushed Patrick's mind. He was quietly going over the fight with his soldiers, pointing out the strengths in Sharne's technique and picking up some of the weaknesses displayed by his own men.

Satisfied they were in good hands, Julianne released her

magic. The steady pace made for a comfortable ride, and she enjoyed being out in this part of the world.

Tahn's weather patterns were different to Arcadia's, and the trees and flowers in the countryside were slightly different. Edging into spring, this was even more obvious than on Julianne's last visit.

Pretty blue flowers stretched over fields, and a giant fig sported glossy purple growth on bare branches. Overhead, puffy white clouds drifted through a flat, blue sky.

Julianne shaded her eyes as she watched them lazily pass, casting shadows on the ground below. She wondered if Bethany Anne really was up there somewhere, still fighting to keep the people of Irth safe from dangers they didn't even know existed.

"What are you dreaming about?" Marcus rode up behind her, startling her with his question.

"Bethany Anne," she admitted. "Also, Hannah. That girl is turning into as much of a legend as the Queen herself."

"It's a new era," Marcus said with a shrug. "We need new heroes. Spunky girls with pet lizards. Old men with scraggly beards." He paused, the corner of his mouth twitching up. "Pretty girls with the power to bring men to their knees."

"And who would that be?" Julianne asked primly.

"You, of course."

Julianne rolled her eyes. "Marcus, I don't deny I can bring men to their knees… but it's not because I'm pretty."

He laughed. "Well, your stunning good looks bring me to my knees."

She did allow herself a chuckle at that. "You're such a romantic. Still, I'd rather have well-honed skills than a nice face. What happens when I get old?"

"What *does* happen when you get old?" Marcus asked seriously.

"What do you mean?" Julianne asked.

"Well, Ezekiel was, like, a thousand years old. Will you live that long?" He let his gaze drift away.

"You're worried I'll leave you when you're old and grey, and I still look twenty?" Julianne pulled her horse closer to his and reached out to grab his hand. "I'll still love you. Even if you get ugly."

"Gee, thanks," Marcus said.

"Besides, Ezekiel is *not* a thousand years old. Just a couple of hundred. I think." She frowned, trying to remember if he'd ever given her an exact number. "And he doesn't look twenty. I might live to a thousand years old, but spend nine-hundred and seventy of them looking like *him*."

Julianne's eyes misted over. Suddenly, she looked like Ezekiel —though she added a few touches to make him look even older than when they'd seen him last. Marcus recoiled in mock horror.

"Will you still love me when I look like this?" she asked, her voice ringing out clear and bright despite her decrepit appearance.

"Uhh... yes?" Marcus didn't sound at all confident. "I mean, old-Julianne I could love. If you actually turned into an old man? Not so sure about that!"

"I knew your love was only skin deep!" she teased, not dropping the illusion.

Marcus didn't answer right away. "Jules, I love you... but, I'm sorry, that's just disturbing."

Julianne giggled and finally dropped the spell. "It's ok. I think I'd have a hard time making out with you if you suddenly looked like Annie."

Marcus sniggered. "I'll keep that in mind. Next time I have a headache and need the night off, I'll ask Bastian to spell me up."

Julianne squealed in outrage and slapped his shoulder. "You beast!"

"You started it!" Marcus laughed.

"Fine! No more Ezekiel mask!" Julianne said. "I like your cute, curly locks just the way they are."

Marcus ran a hand through his hair self-consciously. "They are quite cute, aren't they?"

"Adorable," Bette called from behind. "Just the right length to grab a hold of and lop yer head off, though."

"She's right," Julianne said. "You do need a haircut."

"What?" Marcus protested. "You just said they were cute!"

"They are!" Julianne assured him "But they're also a health risk. We can ask Annie to do it next time we visit. She loves cutting your hair."

Marcus sighed. "I'm not gonna win this one, am I?"

"Nope," Bette called as Julianne shook her head.

Marcus sighed and nudged his horse ahead, leaving Bette and Julianne to ride together.

"Ye look nervous, lass," Bette said gently.

Julianne considered the question. "Just… not sure what to expect. Usually when I'm walking into something, I've seen the important details from someone else's mind. This time, it feels different."

"Ye can't wrap yer head around it, can ye?" Bette nodded to herself. "Aye. Took us all a few visits and a few more drinks to believe it was real. It's not like a fancy buildin' or a new breed of mountain cat. It's an impossible thing, hangin' in the air like nobody's business."

"I think you're right," Julianne said. "My mind keeps trying to come up with explanations, refusing to grasp that the images I've seen are real. And I've seen a lot of things, real and false."

"And ye've made a few of them yerself," Bette reminded her. "But just because ye've seen a lot, doesn't mean ye've seen it all."

"That's the beauty of it, though." Julianne glanced at the bright clouds drifting across the sky again. "No one person ever *will* see it all. Not even the Queen herself."

"The Queen?" Bette asked. "She's seen everything! All those stories, they make it sound like she's been everywhere!"

Julianne raised a finger. "She's not here, is she? She didn't see us free Tahn or fight off Adrien. She doesn't know about his flying machine or our magitech weapons."

Briefly, an image flitted across Julianne's mind. Amongst the barrage of information Hannah had sent, was a view of a large, scaly beast that flew through the air. The emotions that came with it had immediately brought Sal, Hannah's magically-altered pet, to mind. *That flying monstrosity couldn't be the tiny creature Hannah had back in Arcadia... could it?*

Unable to solve that particular mystery while on the road, Julianne banished it from her mind. With all the revelations they'd had in the past few days, nothing seemed impossible anymore.

And if monsters from other worlds and portals through space are possible... what things are we capable of? Things we've never dreamed of? Julianne sat deep in her saddle, allowing her mind to wander for the rest of the journey.

When they turned off the main road to Muir, Julianne forced her mind back to the present. They wove through the forest, taking the newer, wider path that Francis had ordered built.

They passed the school, and Julianne insisted they stop.

"Master! You've come for an inspection?" Bastian took her hand and helped her off the horse.

"I didn't realize you'd made so much progress," Julianne admitted. To be fair, she hadn't been keeping up to date with the new build—too busy with more pressing matters to give the school the attention she wanted to.

"It's going well," Bastian said. "Though, we've had two accidents. No one was hurt, thanks to Jessop's help."

"Jessop?" Julianne hadn't realized the old man was involved in the build.

"He's the only one who knows as much as Francis when it comes to building," Bastian explained. "He insisted on extra bracing in a few areas. That saved lives when a platform came loose one day."

"That doesn't sound normal," Julianne said with a frown.

Bastian shrugged. "We still have no idea how it could have happened. Jessop thinks maybe a beam was flawed or damaged somehow."

"And the other accident?" Julianne pressed.

Bastian blushed. "That was me. I was up top—" he pointed to a narrow boardwalk near the second floor, which was still under construction. "I tripped over my own damn boots and slammed face first into the safety railing."

Julianne shook her head at that. "I'm glad you've got someone to help. I know that construction isn't exactly your area of expertise."

Bastian chuckled. "You mean, you know I'm a klutz, and completely ignorant of the intricacies of building."

Julianne grinned. "I was being polite."

He led her on a brief tour, pointing out gaps in the stone walls that would serve as windows or doors, and showing her the layout of the lowest floor.

"You know," she said, turning a slow circle in the roughly-framed room that would become his office. "There's not a lot of space in here."

"I don't need much to be comfortable," he said.

Julianne laughed. "You may not... but if you remember the gigantic piles of paperwork I had sent to me every day, you'd know why a big office is a gift from the Queen Bitch herself."

Bastian winced. "But you ran a whole Temple. This is..."

"Just a school?" she teased. "You know that's not all this is. You're going to become a center of education, a bastion of all that Arcadia could have been if Adrien wasn't so short-sighted. Combined with talent training? You're breaking new ground, and the whole world will want to know how it's going and will look to you for leadership and advice."

Bastian was pale. "All 1 wanted was to teach some kids, Master. I'm not cut out for *that* kind of responsibility."

She patted his shoulder. "Too late now, my friend. I have faith in you, though. I think you're exactly the right person to do this."

He blew a puff of air through his lips, then mustered a grin. "You've never been wrong before!"

"And you'll have Tansy beside you to keep your feet on the ground. Right?" Julianne looked around and found the performer hanging upside down, legs wrapped around a beam as she secured a rope to it.

Bastian glanced at her, then quickly turned away. "It doesn't matter how many times she does that, I can't watch."

Julianne laughed. "I trust in you. You need to trust in her."

He sighed, then forced himself to watch as Tansy tested her knots, then dropped down onto the rope, grasping it with one hand. She swung out over a wide space, kicked off a beam on the other side, then leveraged her momentum to land on another beam with a quick bow.

A smattering of applause from below made her grin, before tossing the end of the rope around a post. She bent down to secure it, then yelled to a builder on another platform. "Ready!"

The rope became a pulley and soon, a flurry of work had commenced. After watching and breathing in the excitement, Julianne turned to Bastian.

"I'm sorry, Bastian. I can't stay."

"Off to see the rift?" he asked. "Can't deny that's a lot more exciting than my sticks and bricks."

"The potential here shouldn't be underestimated," she said, smiling. "But yes, I need to see the rift. Bastian... is it as strange as it seems?"

He shuddered. "More. I can't explain, though. You'll see."

Brushing off a momentary discomfort at his words, Julianne

left. She pulled herself up onto her horse, nodded to her companions, and began the last leg of the journey.

"Here's the wee bastard," Bette said as they rounded the last bend in the trail.

"Where?" Julianne looked around, intent on seeing the rift for the first time without the interference of anyone else's thoughts.

Bette thrust her chin toward the watchtower. "Over there. Go on."

Julianne dismounted and slowly walked over to the tower. The structure had been placed so that it obscured the view of the rift from the trail, and a line of thick bushes further camouflaged it.

The guards—Sherp, Jarv, and Lewis today—nodded respectfully as she passed. Sherp waved to get her attention.

"If you need to chuck your breakfast, that's the direction you want to aim in." He pointed to a low bush and gave her a wink. "No shame in it. Pretty much everyone has that reaction the first time."

"That bad, then," Julianne murmured.

She pushed aside a flimsy branch and stepped through to the clearing on the other side.

"*Ohh…*" Whatever she'd meant to say was lost in a breathy sigh as she walked closer.

Rustling behind her couldn't pull her attention from the frozen bolt of blackness that absorbed the light around it.

"Careful, Jules," Marcus warned her.

Julianne nodded absentmindedly as she slowly circled around the rift. From the side and back, it didn't exist. It just… vanished. *There*. She caught a glimpse as she came around the other side, and ducked her head back to confirm that, yes, the paper-thin slice twisted and disappeared when viewed from a different angle.

"I'll be damned," she whispered.

Her eyes ached to bring it into focus properly. It hung in the air, its distance difficult to gauge as her eyes struggled to make sense of the startling narrowness that somehow held unfathomable depths.

"It doesn't seem real, does it?" Marcus whispered. He shifted uncomfortably as Julianne stepped closer to it.

"It's ok," she said and held out a hand to settle him. "I won't touch it."

Still, she raised her other hand and held it an inch away from the face of the rift. Her eyes glossed over, and Marcus bent low, ready to tackle her to the ground to break whatever connection she might make.

Julianne's breath caught as Marcus held his. She staggered back, and he rushed forwards, catching her in his arms.

"There's… there's something on the other side," she gasped, pulling away and righting herself.

She stalked over to the rift, eyes clear and face drawn.

"Something, or someone?" Marcus asked.

She shook her head. "It was jumbled. I couldn't tell, but… I think it *saw* me."

CHAPTER SEVENTEEN

Garrett slapped a plate of bread and ham on a rickety table near the watchtower.

"Ye can't be wastin' away, not when the wee beasties are out for yer blood!" He could hear the manic edge to his own voice, but Bitch take his soul if he wasn't pining for another round with the claw-legged bastards.

"And how are ye goin' ta fight with a tummy full of bloat?" Bette jabbed a finger at his middle and laughed.

"It's not fer me, lass. I don't want young Julianne to go hungry, is all." He looked at the table and crossed his fingers that the smell of hot rolls that had been baked fresh in hot coals would somehow pass through the rift and lure the demon spawn through.

"Sit yer ass down and eat," Bette snapped.

"Is everything ok?" Julianne asked, casting a glance between them.

Garrett prickled under the collar. "I'm fine. Fine!" He glared at Bette as he jerked a chair out and sat down hard. *Go on,* he thought. *I dare ye ta disagree.*

Bette shook her head mournfully. "He's anything but fine."

"Bitch," Garrett muttered.

"He's afraid." Bette held a hand out to examine her fingernails. "Poor dear got a right scare when that wee vark tried ta kill Marcus. Shook him up bad, the poor lad."

"I'm *NOT FUCKING SCARED!*" Garrett bellowed, standing up and slamming his hands on the table.

Silence fell over the camp, and all eyes turned to him.

Garrett cast a nervous glance around, then slowly sat. "I'm *not* scared," he repeated quietly.

"It's alright, love," Bette said soothingly. "We know ye were just scared for Marcus's sake."

Marcus opened his mouth to speak, then yelped. He leaned down to rub his ankle under the table, studiously avoiding Garrett's glare.

"Yeah," Marcus said. "For me. I was scared, too, dammit!"

Garrett barked a laugh. "Ye were fuckin' terrified, weren't ye? But we'll show the pricks. Next time they come through, we'll stab their beady wee eyes, and gut the bastards, and spread their entrails over the camp. We'll show 'em!"

"Aye, love." Bette patted his arm. "We'll spread 'em all over. Now, have a roll."

Garrett shoved a bite into his mouth, and promptly choked on it. Coughing and wheezing, he grabbed Bette's arm, mouth open like a fish flopping on the floor of a boat.

"I'll get ye some water, dear." Bette stood far too slowly for his liking, but went towards the watchtower, where the drinking water was stored. "Err... Julianne, can ye help?"

Garrett's eyes prickled, and bile rose in his throat. With a mighty heave, the lump of soggy bread shot out of his mouth and across the table. Marcus lurched out of its way, then prodded the offending lump with the end of his fork.

Garrett lurched to his feet.

"What are—" Marcus asked, then quieted when Garrett waved a hand to shush him.

Ignoring Marcus's curious gaze, Garrett stumbled over towards the tower, as quietly as he could, despite the burning urge to cough.

"...and he just hasn't been right since," Bette was saying inside.

Garrett crouched, stuffing a hand into his mouth and biting down to stop the tickle in his throat.

"I could try and soothe some of his fear," Julianne replied. "But sometimes using that particular spell on a rearick can—oh, dear."

Julianne's bright face popped out of the doorway. "Didn't your mother tell you it's rude to eavesdrop?" she scolded Garrett.

"My m—" Garrett felt his throat seize and wracking coughs overtook him. He gasped and started again, snatching the waterskin from Bette when she joined Julianne beside him.

"Ye traitorous bitch!" He wheezed. "I'm not fuckin' scared, I'm *tellin'* ye!"

"I know, Garrett." Julianne placed a gentle hand on his shoulder and looked deep into his eyes, her own fading to white.

He tried to jerk away, but instead of a false calm, he felt understanding. He felt Julianne's own fear—not for herself, but for the people she'd sworn to protect, for her friends, and especially for Marcus.

He felt her fear shift. Not changing, but evolving, leading to a burning desire to crush any threat that faced the people she loved.

"I *know*," she said when her eyes cleared.

Garrett leaned his back against the wall. "Aye," he said in a croaky voice. "I suppose ye do."

"Och, we all know yer a pussy," Bette said with a grin. "But I prefer ye to be a *breathin'* pussy. Next time, chew yer bloody food."

Garrett stuck his tongue out at her, but let the two women guide him back to the table.

Over lunch, they talked of many things. The battle for Arcadia and the one for Tahn; the Heights, the city, and the weather. They danced around the topic of the rift and the threat that faced them but did so comfortably and without fear.

Finally, when the food was gone, and they all leaned back to enjoy the hazy relaxation that always comes after a good meal, Bette sighed.

"If yer stayin' until we get another visitor ta pop through, ye might be here a good while." She wiped her hands on her shirt. "Ye may as well get comfortable."

As it turned out, the wait wasn't too long at all. Just on dusk, while Garrett was resting his eyelids under the same table they'd lunched at, a cry went up from the bushes.

Garrett bolted upright, cursing as his head made contact with the table. "Fuck!" He grabbed at his axe, lying nearby, and rolled out. Jumping to his feet, he whooped a war cry as he raced for the rift.

Julianne was already there, staff gripped in two hands as she watched the edges of the portal shift and bend.

"Wait for it…" Garrett growled, excitement building. Blood pounded in his ears and raced through his veins. "Come on, laddies. Give old uncle Garrett another shot at yer faces, eh?"

"Don't scare it off," Marcus said. "And can you try to let me get a shot in, too? I still owe them a good belting after last time."

"Och, ye'll be hard pressed to find an opening once I start swingin'," Garrett said with a wolfish smile. His eyes drank in the low light of the evening, riveted on the wobbling line before them.

First one arm, then another crawled through. The rest of the creature fell through with a slurping pop.

"What's that?" Julianne snapped, pointing.

At first, it looked like the beast's leg had gotten stuck. Then…

"It's bringin' a friend!" Garrett screeched, exhilaration smoking him. He launched forwards, twirling his weapon towards the stick-like creature half his height.

"Garrett, stop!" Julianne called.

Garrett froze mid-stride. He looked at her white eyes and snarled. "This isn't a time for mind-fuckin', it's time to splatter some guts!" He whipped his axe forwards and, as he'd expected, it glanced off the hard carapace on his target's back.

Another slice slipped between the hard coverings on the upper and lower legs, neatly chopping a leg in half. A thin wail pierced his ears, and he dropped the weapon, grabbing at his ears.

The second alien shot straight at Marcus, but was knocked back by a hard, swift swing of Julianne's staff. It fell back, but landed on its stalk-like legs, immediately hurling itself back towards her.

Garrett threw himself at the whining beast, landing in a puff of dry dirt.

Roaring to drown out the high-pitched noise, Garrett let go of his head. He scooped his axe up and edged around, one of the beast's eye-stalks following him closely.

It jumped, and Garrett quickly followed suit leaping after it. Man and tiny beast connected, and Garrett felt the barbed hooks latch into his chest.

"I've got ye now, ye dick-eye'd wee cockroach!" Garrett thrust an arm up to protect his face, then grabbed one of the creature's eyes. He yanked it out, roaring again as the painful scream intensified.

He shoved it to the ground and smashed the flat head of his axe into its gut. Ichor and grainy slime splattered out, and he pounded again, ignoring the stench and stickiness that covered him.

Over and over, he brought his axe down on the beast, pounding it into a pile of sticky, brittle shards. Then, he raised his axe to smash down on a leg... and froze.

His body seized, held still except his lungs and eyes. He heaved sharp breaths, rolling his eyes around to see what had him.

Julianne stood over him, looking down with white eyes.

"We good?" she asked.

"Errrgghhh." His lips and tongue were still frozen.

"Garrett, I'm in your head. I heard that." She waited, and Garrett relented.

Sorry. Shouldn't have called ye a bossy tart. Not even in me head.

His muscles released, and he collapsed, face plunging into a pile of acrid alien blood.

"Pah! Ack, blerch!"

"Ye shouldn't'a made such a Bitch-damned mess," Bette scolded. "Who knows what kind of scavengers all that blood will bring? Last thing we need here is rats."

"Rats?" Garrett felt a bubble of laughter rise in his chest. "Rats? Yer worried about *rats*?" He fell back to the ground, laughing hysterically.

Through his mirth, he heard Bette sigh.

"He's just a wee bit wound up. He'll be fine."

Marcus leaned down to grasp his forearm and pull him to his feet. Sobering, Garrett looked him over. "The other one is dead?"

Marcus nodded. "They go down fast if you slip between the armored bits." He glanced at the mess at Garrett's feet. "Or, I guess, if you pound them to dust."

"Aye," Garrett said, a smile cracking his face wide again. "Easier than dealing with rats!"

"Garrett!" Julianne snapped. Her eyes glowed in the darkness, and Garrett flinched, expecting another mind-trick.

Instead, her eyes cleared. Worry etched her face. "The school. *GO!*"

The fear in her voice sent Garrett's feet running before his mind caught up. Bastian would be at the school—he often worked late. Had a monster slipped through the portal unseen, and attacked the school?

His feet pounded the road, echoing heavy beats behind him.

He spared a glance behind and saw Marcus, racing towards him on horseback with one arm extended.

Garrett grabbed the offered hand, swinging up onto the horse effortlessly.

"How'd the shits get past us?" Garrett called, wind snatching at his words.

"Not them." Marcus shook his head. "*Remnant.*"

A tight band Garrett hadn't noticed around his chest eased. Remnant were a vicious enemy, but they were an enemy he knew well.

The sound of fighting quickly reached them. Marcus dashed the horse into the clearing and waited until Garrett had landed on the ground before vaulting off himself. He yanked the horse back around and slapped its rump, trusting the animal to head back to the rift.

Ahead, bedlam reigned. Remnant tore at stone and wood, shoving hard enough to tumble a half-built wall. Others clustered around a small section, where a room with four walls was almost complete.

"In there," Marcus said, pointing. "I think there are people in there."

"Yargh!" Garrett hollered, gripping his axe in two hands.

"Yargh?" Marcus asked.

Garrett grinned and nodded. "*YARGH!*" He plunged forwards, hurling himself right in the middle of the remnant trying to break down a flimsy door.

A hand grabbed his shirt, and he spun, lopping it off. Another flew at his face, knuckles cracking loudly as they connected with the haft of his axe.

"Help!" A feminine scream that was muffled by solid stone walls reached Garrett's ears, and he fought harder, shoving his way through to press his back against the door.

"COME AT ME YE ROTTIN' LIMP DICKED MUD EATERS!"

The remnant around him paused, as if startled at his sudden threat. Then, as one, they descended.

Garrett clenched his teeth, whipping his axe with lethal precision. He spun, dodging a blow, then ducked to avoid another. He took a fist on the chin and repaid the attacker with an axe to the temple.

Bodies fell, piling at his feet. Remnant climbed over each other, their prey drive overriding any concept of fear, despite the carnage Garrett was laying into them.

Something grabbed his foot, and he stumbled, going down on one knee just as a rusted sword plunged into the wood behind him.

The remnant with the weapon tried to jerk it back, but it stuck fast. Garrett barked a laugh as he twisted the wrist of the beast who had tripped him, feeling the satisfying crunch of broken bones. He stood

"*DUCK!*"

Garrett threw himself back down at Marcus's cry, hooting in joy as blood rained down, and a head tumbled at his feet.

Instead of standing, he spun low, ploughing his axe through two legs and sinking into the calf of a third. When the remnant stumbled, he punched it in the face, sinking his fist far enough in to tickle what brain it had left.

Garrett looked around. The remnant were starting to retreat. "Not today, ye unlucky bastards!" He had to climb over a stack of bodies, slipping in fresh blood.

Thinking he was unbalanced, a remnant rushed him. He dispatched it with a lazy flick of his blade. He quickly noted Marcus running down a fleeing beast and turned the other way, hurling his axe into the back of a skull.

A noise above, followed by another shriek, alerted him to more danger. Three remnant had scaled the walls and were trying to pry the upper level floorboards apart.

Garrett frantically looked but couldn't see any way to get up there.

"Marcus!" he yelled. "I need a wee boost, ye lazy shit!"

Marcus pulled his sword out of a limp body and looked up. He glanced at Garrett, then at the three desperate beasts above the rearick. "Be right there."

Marcus ran, sword gripped tight. Garrett crouched. Marcus slid to a stop on one knee, hands interlocked.

Garrett jumped. He landed well, planting one foot in Marcus's hands. Marcus heaved, thrusting upwards and rocketing Garrett towards the sky.

Garrett used his strong legs to propel him and flew high enough to grab the top edge of the building. Unfortunately, his hands were slick with fresh blood.

He slipped. A brief trip through the air ended with a hard smack on the dirt. Marcus looked down from above him and shrugged.

Garrett vaulted to his feet in time to see Marcus wrench the door open. Tansy and Bastian tumbled out, faces white.

Garrett grinned. He slipped into the room and quietly shut the door behind him.

Inside, light seeped through the cracks overhead, highlighting the shadows of the moving remnant. With a groan, one of the floorboards gave way.

Shrieking in delight, the remnant dropped down. Garrett grinned as, one by one, their eyes adjusted to the dim room.

"*Surprise!*"

He lashed out, slicing across with his axe and feeling it bite into soft flesh and organs. Guts spilled as the last remnant whispered a single word. "Fuck." Moments later, the life in its glowing red eyes flickered out.

Garrett planted a foot against the door and shoved. Outside, Tansy dropped a limp remnant to the ground while Marcus watched approvingly.

AMY HOPKINS & MICHAEL ANDERLE

"Holy shit," she gasped. "You guys got here just in time."

"It looked like ye were about to become dinner," Garrett agreed.

Tansy laughed. "Not that. I just didn't want to miss *my* dinner. It would have taken ages to fight them all off ourselves!"

Garrett couldn't do anything but laugh at the girl's plucky courage. "Aye," he said. "It would have taken ye a wee while."

"Where did they come from?" Marcus asked, kicking at a twitching body. He leaned down to run his sword through it, and it fell still.

Bastian sat, hands trembling. "I don't know. They just rushed in all at once, screaming. We barely had time to find cover."

"You might need to rethink being here alone," Marcus suggested.

Bastian quickly nodded. "Don't you worry, I'm not coming out here without an armed guard from now on."

Tansy pouted. "You don't think I could have taken them?"

Bastian threw his hands up. "Sure! You against thirty slavering ghouls. But like you said, we'd have missed dinner."

Tansy flung her arms around him. "I love that you believe in me!" She landed a wet kiss on his cheek. "But realistically, we'd have been dead in about twelve seconds. I didn't even have a weapon!"

"How'd ye take down that one?" Garrett asked, using his axe to point at the body at her feet.

"Quick head twist," she said. "I can show you if you like?"

Garrett gave her a mournful look. "Lass, I'm not tall enough to wring a neck like that!"

Tansy giggled. "Then you've got to lop it off at the knees, first!"

Garrett stretched, realizing he felt calmer than he had in days. "Ah, nothin' like a good tousle with some dead heads to calm the nerves."

Marcus snorted. "If you say so. Do you two want to head back to town, or come with us?"

Tansy looked at Garrett and wrinkled her nose. "We probably shouldn't walk back in the dark, alone. Where is the nearest place ol' Garrett here can take a bath?"

"What?" Garrett sniffed loudly. "I can't smell a thing!"

"You're the only one here who can't," Bastian said, pulling his head back away from the rearick. "What is that? It doesn't smell like remnant blood."

"It's vark," Garrett said with a smirk.

Tansy squealed. "You didn't! Those adorable little balls?"

"Ack, no. More like a… super-vark. A vark-sect?" Garrett pursed his lips, thinking. "Insectovark!"

"He went a little crazy when one of the nasty ones came through the rift," Marcus explained. "Come on. Julianne is waiting for us back at the rift. There's a horse trough there we can tip over stink-guts here."

They walked back together, quiet in the deepening twilight. When they returned to the camp, Julianne greeted them with a heavy bucket.

Garrett eyed it warily. "What's that f—"

Julianne tipped it over his head, sloshing water down his face and drowning out his words. "You stink, Garrett. And if you don't clean that off, I'll make you spend the next three weeks thinking you can smell dogshit on your boots."

"Oh, fine." He laughed and shook off the droplets, then made his way to the trough of clean water.

As he stripped off his shirt, Bette leaned over the railing at the top of the watchtower. She gave a loud whistle. "Hello, sexy! Ye feel better after yer little adventure?"

"Aye!" Garrett called, drubbing grime off his bristling chest. "Feel like a real man again! Ye want to know what a real man feels like?" He unbuttoned his pants, sending Julianne and Tansy running inside, screaming and giggling.

"Ach, they don't know what they're missin'," Bette hollered down.

"We don't want to find out, thanks!" Tansy yelled from inside.

Garrett dropped his pants to scrub off the last of the grime. Marcus raised a hand over his eyes. "I'm blind!"

"Ah, ye jealous, lad?" Garrett bellowed a laugh.

"Oh, for Bitch's sake," Sherp yelled from the rift. "Has Garrett got his pants off again? Stop scaring the wildlife, man!"

Garrett, skin shining clean and white in the moonlight, flashed a sparkling grin. Then, he took off, sprinting for the rift, naked as the day he was born. "Yer just jealous I've still got both me balls!" he yelled. "I'll show ye what a real man looks like!"

Inside, Bette landed on the ground floor of the tower. "Looks like me man is back to his usual happy self," she said with a grin.

"Yes," Julianne said. She shook her head slowly. "I'm glad... but I wish he wasn't quite so happy as that."

CHAPTER EIGHTEEN

Bastian squinted against the glare as the heavy beam carefully dropped into place.

"How are you doing, Jakob?" he asked once it was secure.

Jakob's eyes cleared from black to brown, and he smiled weakly. "Feels great! I've been getting lazy in Muir, living off pastries and being waited on hand and foot."

"I know that's a lie," Bastian laughed. "I don't need magic to tell you feel like a used ass-wipe. Even Lord George was worried you were going to burn yourself out with all the repairs and building you've been helping with."

Jakob's laugh was interrupted by a growling burp. "I really haven't done that much. Some buildings in the lower end of town were badly neglected for a while. They just needed some patching up, and I wasn't the only one getting his hands dirty."

"And the patrols?" Bastian probed. He knew Jakob was one of those who spent nights manning the walls of Muir to guard against the increasing number of remnant attacks.

"Rarely more than an excuse for a long game of cards with a nice view." Jakob's eyes clouded over with the color of midnight, and he turned back to the building site.

"Huh." Bastian let the matter slide as he watched the magic user painstakingly lift another heavy beam into the air. Jakob didn't just look worn out—he looked like he was going to deposit his breakfast on his own boots.

The post hovered, then carefully inched up to the upper platform where three men stood, waiting with outstretched hands. They grabbed the beam as soon as it was close enough, but Bastian noticed a tell-tale wobble as it was lowered.

"Jakob, seriously." He turned to the other man, who gave him an embarrassed grin. "If you need to take a break, we can keep going for a while without you. There's plenty to keep us busy."

Jakob ducked his head. "Alright. I was going to rest for a bit after the next one anyway."

"Samuel!" Bastian called. "Jakob's off for a bit. Can you secure the new beams? Make sure the railings are tight first—I don't want anyone falling overboard."

"Sure, boss," Samuel yelled back. "As soon as these pussies finish pulling the splinters from their delicate little hands."

"Hey, it's the size of a fucking nail!" Taven called, lingering out of sight up above. "It's a pisser, too!"

A hand darted out over the edge, squeezed into a fist. A steady dribble of tiny red droplets spattered on the ground.

"Hey!" Bastian yelped. "That's fresh-cut pine you're bleeding on!"

The hand disappeared, and a chagrined 'sorry' sounded from the upper level.

Bastian cursed and leaned down to inspect the damage. A messy stain covered one of the planks and dripped down the side.

The boards were to cover his office walls. Though he'd increased his floor plan on Julianne's advice, he still intended to keep the room plain. To him, that meant comfortable.

"Pre-loved torture chamber isn't exactly the look I was going for," he muttered as he scrubbed at the mark with his sleeve. "Pigs balls! It's already soaked in."

As he straightened, the ground rumbled below his feet. Bastian jerked his head up, eyes locking on the structure above.

The upper level wavered and shook. He scurried backwards, tripping over his robe in his rush to get away. "Brace!" he screamed. "Brace yourselves!"

The building collapsed. Dust clouds rose from the wreckage, stinging Bastian's eyes. Over the creak of settling timber, he heard screams.

Immediately, he reached out with his magic. He grit his teeth as his mind locked onto the workers. His pain sensors went into overdrive as their agony flooded into him, and he hunched, trying to center himself and temper the sensation.

My legs. My legs, I can't feel them.

IthurtsithurtsithurtsohgodI'mdying.

Wha—what happened...

Bastian sorted through the mental ramblings of the fallen men as other workers rushed towards the wreckage. As they started pulling posts and boards free, one of his mind-connections wobbled.

"*STOP!*" Bastian screamed. "Stop! It's unstable! Samuel's trapped under there."

The men jumped back as Jakob stumbled over, face pale.

"Bitch strike me!" He gasped. "I thought the noise was just my guts turning over!"

"What?" Bastian looked over and saw the wet stain on Jakob's shirt.

Jakob closed his eyes and rested a hand on his stomach. "I knew I wasn't right—I don't normally get tired that fast. Guess I shouldn't have eaten that ham for breakfast. It smelled funny, but I thought I'd..." he turned and vomited on the ground.

"Fuck a dead remnant," Bastian groaned. "Jakob, go home. You can't use magic in that condition."

Jakob squared his shoulders and made to protest, but Bastian cut him off.

"Three men are trapped. One wrong move, and they'll be crushed. I can't afford mistakes, Jakob."

Jakob spat the sour taste out of his mouth. "Fair enough. But I can still ride—I'll send for help."

Bastian gave a short nod as Jakob ran off, the other man already banished from his thoughts. Bastian could still feel the pain of the fallen men, but it had faded to a dull throb. Their fear prickled at his soul, though.

Stay calm, he thought, sending out a wave of comfort and security. The fear ebbed a little, but Taven's thoughts drifted further away. The man had a head injury, Bastian was sure of it.

It made the situation even more urgent. "Right!" Bastian barked. "We're going to take off one beam at a time. Carefully!"

Summoning every ounce of concentration, he reached out to Jessop and Andy. Once his mind had connected with theirs, he pointed. "These two will do the lifting. No one else is to touch the rubble—just be ready to take pieces off them when they ask."

The remaining four men clustered around. Carefully, Jessop and Andy lifted a long pole.

I don't have the energy to talk, Bastian explained. *But I'll guide you.*

Bastian sent another wave of calmness towards Samuel and Jayne, dampening their panic as they felt the rubble pinning them begin to shift.

He nudged Jessop away from a beam that shifted the pile, pressing down on Samuel's torso. When a different plank relieved pressure on Jayne's arm, Bastian felt Jessop and Andy strain to lift it.

He pushed out a short, sharp breath, then reached his magic out to a fifth man. *Help them*, he sent to Lior.

With a start, Lior jumped in and grabbed Jessop's end of the beam. Together, they levered it up and shifted it to the right.

No, left! Bastian sent urgently. The men changed direction and pulled off the beam. *Hold it—HOLD it!* He sent a burst of determination towards them.

Free... Jayne saw his chance and pulled himself towards the opening, then collapsed back as pain engulfed him. *Ohfuckohfuck-ohfuck.* Despair clustered in around the agony as tears streamed down the man's face.

Bastian's own eyes began to leak as Jayne's helplessness reached him. *You can do this*, Bastian sent.

Barely aware of the voice in his head, Jayne groaned. *Can't move. Hurts.*

I'll help, Bastian sent. *You have to move. Now!*

The men above heaved deep breaths as they held the large beam still as Bastian whispered a spell to take away the sharp, biting pain in Jayne's leg.

Normally, that would go against every rule the Temple had taught. Taking away the body's ability to recognize pain meant a man could exceed normal limits—leading to further injury.

If Jayne didn't move, he would die under the stack of planks and pillars. *Go. Now!* Bastian gasped a word through gritted teeth and filled Jayne with urgency, a feeling so strong it overrode his fear and despair.

Jayne scrambled out, dragging one limp limb behind him. As soon as he was free, Jessop, Lior, and Andy lowered the beam with shaking hands.

"No time to rest, boys," Bastian said. "We've got two more men to free."

I'm sorry, Samuel, Bastian sent. *Taven is losing consciousness, we have to get him out first.*

Reading the resolute patience in the team leader's mind, Bastian sighed with relief. Samuel was in pain and gripped by the same fear every worker would know facing death, but he put his friend's lives first.

Keep them safe. Bastian heard the wisp of thought just as he withdrew from Samuel's mind.

I will, Sam, Bastian thought to himself. He steadied his lock on Taven's thoughts, a task growing harder by the minute as the man's mind wandered farther and farther away.

Stay awake, Taven! Bastian snapped in the man's head. A startled Taven responded with thoughts of his father yelling at him for daydreaming.

Bastian hurried his workers along, ushering them into position. The strain of holding the three workers and forcing Taven's mind to stay conscious sent biting spearheads into his temples. "Lior, just follow the others. Don't grab anything before they do."

He let go of the spell that linked him with Lior, letting him see through the man's eyes and communicate with him by feel.

"Right." Bastian took a moment to center himself—a difficult process while holding so many mental threads. "Start at the top," he directed Jessop.

The old man gave a quick jerk of his head and gingerly pulled at a wee sheet of board. Bastian carefully cradled Taven's mind, letting himself feel what the trapped man felt.

The space he was trapped in was musty and smelled of damp soil. Bright pricks of light scored his eyes where sunlight peeked through gaps. His skin shuddered and trembled as the rubble pressing his flesh was disturbed.

"Not that one," Bastian whispered.

His speech was reflexive—the thought behind the words was sent directly into Jessop's mind. "Yes. Careful…"

The ache of burning so much magic, stretching his mind so far while inflicting it with the agony of the injured men, prickled at his skin. He fought for control.

Taven's world shuddered and slipped as a stack of planks slid off the pile, freeing him.

As the pressure faded from his body, Taven slipped away.

Bastian collapsed. "No…" Kneeling in the dirt, he stretched

for Taven... and didn't find him. Bastian prayed the man was only unconscious.

Jessop nudged his shoulder. "You ok there, mystic? Still a man to go."

Bastian nodded. He clenched his fists and cleared his mind, reveling in the brief lapse that let his mental muscles drop the burden for just a few moments. "Samuel."

The name grounded him, brought images of the man as Bastian had last seen him. Coarse and surly, running his small building team with a no-nonsense approach. A strong work ethic had etched lines into Samuel's tanned face and built muscles that looked more suited to a man half his age.

Bastian muttered a word and reached for the mind that matched the image in his head. Samuel ached with a resignation that broke his heart—the man had already accepted his likely death.

"Jessop," Bastian whispered.

Beside him, someone stepped forwards. The scent of fresh-cut pine, stale ink, and fresh sweat reached his nostrils. Yes, that was Jessop.

The cavalry has arrived! Need a hand?

Danil's silent voice washed over Bastian like a cool balm, filling his body with life and energy. The razed nerves in his head calmed, easing the searing pain.

Bastian nodded, knowing Danil would see it no matter how far he was.

Closing his eyes and working purely by the sight and feel of the two men he held in his spell, Bastian put Jessop to work.

One beam came free, then another. When Jessop tugged at a third, Bastian sent a blast of control, freezing him into stillness.

Jessop carefully turned his head and worked his mouth. Bastian let him, but held the muscles from his neck down in a tight grip. "How bad?" he asked in a low voice.

"That beam," Bastian said, just loud enough for the man and

those around him to hear. "It's holding everything. If you move it an inch…"

He didn't need to finish the sentence. They knew what would happen if the pile collapsed.

Danil's consciousness slid around Bastian's mind, carefully evaluating the situation. *There's only one way to save him*, Danil sent. *I'm sending in Sir Puke-a-lot.*

Danil pulled a tendril of Bastian's mind along with him, gently draping it over Jakob's mind. Bastian had to throw up a hurried mental shield to stop Jakob's nausea emptying his stomach.

Sorry. Despite the tension, Danil's voice held a thread of laughter. *Should have warned you about that…*

"Jessop, don't move," Bastian called. "But when I give you the signal, get the hell out of the way!"

Jessop nodded.

Unfolding images in Jakob's mind, Bastian showed him Samuel's predicament.

Jakob's face screwed up in concentration. "I've got this." He blew out three fast breaths.

The pile of rubble exploded. It shot in the air, hung still for a moment, then swept off to one side, slamming against a partially collasped wall before crashing to the ground.

Jessop staggered and fell backwards. Bastian's tenuous link with him meant he felt the sharp crack as a post clipped the old man's chin. It hurt, but not enough to worry about Jessop's safety.

Bastian rushed forward, his spells falling away. Samuel's body lay on the dirt, in a barren circle surrounded by wood and debris.

"Sam!" Bastian yelled, skidding along the dirt on his knees. He stumbled to a stop at the team leader's side.

Samuel propped himself up on one elbow. "Bitch's oath," he muttered. "That's one way to clear a mess."

The sounds of violent vomiting erupted behind them. Bastian

winced, and swallowed to keep his sympathetic stomach from turning.

"How's Taven?" Samuel asked.

Bastian glanced back over his shoulder. To his surprise, he saw Rhea bent over, tending to the two injured men with Mathias watching over her. The girl's training was far from complete, but he knew she at least had *some* healing ability.

"He'll be just fine," Bastian said with a grin.

Samuel's face wrinkled.

"Are you hurt?" Bastian asked quickly. "I'll get Rhea over to—"

"I'm fine," Samuel said grumpily. "But this Bitch-damned worksite is a mess! Look at those men, standing around like starved fish. This isn't a tits and ass convention!" He yelled at some watching workers. "Clean this shit up before someone trips over it."

CHAPTER NINETEEN

Marcus kicked at the gnawed stump that jutted out of the ground. He'd come to the building site with Julianne, the rushed trip made at Danil's request. The damage had been obvious once the fallen debris had been cleared away.

"I don't know what made those teeth marks, but I don't want to meet it in a dark alley," he said.

Francis glanced over and nodded. "Bastian, you've seen nothing?"

Bastian shook his head tiredly. Julianne, one hand on the back of his neck and her own eyes shining bright white as she examined him, clicked her tongue. "Stay still!" she chided.

"Only the little varks," Bastian said. "It would take one weeks to chew through a beam that size, let alone five of them."

"Nah, tiny teeth like that would leave different marks," Jessop insisted. "This was a big'un. Not even a vark the size of a bear's apples would do that."

"Bears apples?" Marcus queried, looking at Bastian.

"Balls," he said. "He means a bear's balls."

"Well, if you want to be unimaginative about it," Jessop sighed.

"Not even the stick creatures that are coming through the

portal could do this," Francis said. He bent down at one of the other damaged posts—this one hadn't been chewed all the way through but had snapped, leaving sharp splinters protruding into the air.

Jakob sauntered over. "Let me at it. I'll take the bastard out."

"With your smell?" Marcus called.

Francis edged backwards. "Most definitely. Any creature that comes near the mighty Jakob would die in a single breath." He pulled his shirt up over his face.

Jakob shrugged and grinned but backed off. "At least I'm not tossing my lunch anymore. Nice of you to catch, though Mathias."

A shirtless Mathias leaned against a tree. "Fuck you. Seriously. That was my best fucking shirt! Next time, you can shove your rotten spew-inducing ham up your—"

"I said sorry!" Jakob protested. "It's not like I could help it."

"You could have aimed better," Mathias grumbled.

"I know you two are having fun," Julianne broke in. "But we need to think of the implications. Something is running about, eating through solid posts. What if it's in Tahn or Muir?"

Silence fell as the men digested her words.

"We'd best head home," Mathias said with a glance at Jakob.

Jakob nodded. "We'll inform Lord George. You'll stay in touch?"

Francis nodded. "We'll send messengers."

"I'm coming back with you," Rhea said. She blushed when everyone's eyes turned to her. "I can send Tabitha faster than any messenger."

Tabitha? Marcus wondered.

Julianne sent the answer in a series of images, thoughts, and memories. They were getting better at communicating this way —to Julianne, it was almost like talking to another mystic, though Marcus couldn't initiate the conversation himself.

She showed him that Tabitha was a small, orange fox. The

animal had adopted Rhea while she was practicing her newfound skill on it, their bond deepening while Rhea trained her nature magic with Mathias.

Now, the animal acted as Rhea's familiar, though Mathias had mentioned the bond was different to those he'd seen back home.

Mathias and Jakob said a subdued farewell and left together. Once they were gone, Francis took in a deep breath, then gagged.

"Oh, Bastard. Shouldn't have done that." There were still several puddles of regurgitated bile in the grass nearby.

"I'm just glad Jakob came back," Bastian said. "Samuel wouldn't have made it out if he hadn't."

"You were doing great!" Danil exclaimed, clapping Bastian on the back. "The level of skill and depth of power you displayed was… well, dare I say it… almost as good as I'd have done!"

Bastian punched Danil lightly on the shoulder.

"Just remember to take it easy for a few days," Julianne reminded Bastian. "You were pushing right up against your limit there. I don't need you burning out on me, ok?"

Bastian nodded, then winced. "With a head like this, I don't think I'll even be tempted to cast a spell anytime soon."

"A head as ugly as that *should* ache," Danil quipped. "Anyway, there's nothing we can do here. I'm going back to Tahn before I lose any appetite I have left."

He swung around and planted a foot down with a wet squelch. Danil froze.

"Uhh… guys?" A sickly green color washed over his face. "Tell me I didn't just stand in Jakob's breakfast."

"What the fuck is that smell? Ye been guttin' week-old fish here or somethin'?" Bette stomped up the trail towards Danil, Garrett following close behind.

She looked down. "Ye seem to have a bit o' chuck on yer boots, lad."

Danil fled, and Julianne had to shield against the wave of sympathetic nausea that trailed behind him.

139

"Bette, I'm glad you came," Julianne said. "Sorry about the stink—Jakob's breakfast didn't agree with him."

"Agree with him?" Garrett chortled. "It looks like it beat him up from the inside, then punched him in the face on the way out."

"Please," Marcus gasped, one hand over his nose and mouth. "I've been sucking in that stink for an hour. If we keep talking about it, I'm going to join him."

"Just my luck to be stuck with a bunch of sympathetic spewers," Julianne said. "But we *do* have more important things to talk about. Come and look at the damage to those posts."

She led the rearick over to the chewed beams. "Do you have any idea what could have done this?"

"Beaver," Garrett said proudly. "Did I get it right?"

Julianne shook her head. "Not this much damage. It was fine yesterday, and two have been cut right through."

"Are ye thinkin' our wee rift bastards are the culprits?" Bette asked. "Surely they'd be too small." She chewed her lip, then darted a glance at Garrett.

Garrett caught the look and sucked on a wisp of beard, frowning.

"You know something," Julianne stated flatly.

"Well... not really," Garrett began.

Julianne raised her eyebrows. "Then tell me what you 'don't really' know."

"Well, we didn't really believe him, ye see," Bette began.

"Aye. Gerard was already toshed when he said he saw it—" Garrett butted in.

"And ye know how Gerard is, eh? Shitfaced an hour after his shift and can't remember his own way home," Bette finished.

They both fell silent.

"And what did Gerard possibly, but maybe not see?" Julianne prodded.

"A vark!" Garrett said.

Julianne frowned, waiting. When no response seemed imminent, she said, "Varks have been coming through for weeks. What was special about *this* vark?"

"Oh, yeah!" Bette exclaimed. "He said it were big as a wee dog. Or, he said a 'wee little dog' but he did this with his hands." She raised her hands above her head to indicate an object quite a bit taller than herself. "That'd be a pretty bloody big dog."

"And he couldn't even tell us if it were a wee dog," Garrett said, levelling his hand as high as his knee, "Or a big fuckin' beast." He raised his hands like Bette had.

"So, what did you do?" Marcus asked. He had his hands on his hips and a stern expression.

Bette shrugged. "We went for a look. There was no sign of a wee-giant beastie. No footprints, but it was rainin', so maybe they washed away. No branches broken, nothin' disturbed."

Garrett shook his head. "I don't think Gerard's imaginary friend was the cause of the damage here, lass. He's a good man and was a fine soldier, but when a man has his snout in a vat of rum, there's no tellin' what he'll think he sees."

"He *was* a good soldier?" Julianne asked.

"Aye." Bette's face dropped. "It gutted the poor bastard, but he knew the bloody rule. No booze when yer on a shift. We don't even allow it near the rift—last thing we need is a bunch of drunks stumbling around if a real wee-giant beastie pops through."

Marcus sighed. "She's right, Jules. Any soldier worth his salt knows not to mix drink and duty."

"Fair enough," Julianne said. "But I still think there might be something to this. I need to speak to Gerard."

They headed back towards the horses, though Bastian took some coaxing to leave the flat rock he was comfortably leaning on.

"Come on, Bastian," Julianne urged. "You'll feel better once you've got a nice, soft mattress under you."

He allowed her to help him stand but couldn't resist throwing one last glance back at the carnage that had been the beginnings of his new school.

"Julianne…" he began, then shook his head. "Never mind."

"What is it?" she asked, hesitant to dive into his mind after it had been so overworked.

He paused again, looking towards the chewed-up stumps. "The posts that were damaged… it was only four. And only the four that could cause an accident like that. Any other beam or post, and it wouldn't have caused anything like that…"

A cold shudder crawled down Julianne's back. "You think those spots were targeted deliberately?"

Bastian laughed nervously. "Crazy, right? Guess I lost a few screws when I pushed too hard."

Julianne wrapped an arm around his shoulder. "I trust your instincts, Bastian. You should, too."

He gave her a wavering smile before climbing on her horse. Julianne mounted behind him and called to Marcus, who was waiting patiently ahead. "Ready to go?"

Marcus grinned and kicked his horse.

"Now," Julianne muttered, glad to have a course of action ahead. "Let's go speak to Gerard."

CHAPTER TWENTY

Gerard opened the door, his eyes bright and clear but shadowed by dark rings.

"Master Julianne! Master Bastian, please, do come in."

He ushered the mystics past without greeting Marcus—to the soldier, he just ducked his head and scurried away.

Inside, Gerard's little cottage was immaculately clean, if a little drab around the edges. His ageing curtains had moth-eaten holes in them, and the old table he gestured for them to sit at had scratches and bumps from years of use.

Despite the worn appearance of his decor, nothing sat out of place. A set of open shelves framing the window displayed carefully stacked crockery that sparkled in the afternoon light filtering through the spotless glass of the window.

Even the faded rug was free of dirt. The scent of fresh lemons prickled Julianne's nose.

"Who does your cleaning?" she asked, impressed.

Gerard chuckled awkwardly. "Me, Master. Last ten days I've been... Well, I guess you know I'm off the guard. But I've been cleaning up, in more ways than one." His eyes slid towards

Marcus and quickly darted away again. Then, he heaved a deep and meaningful sigh.

"You've been keeping yourself busy, then," Marcus said with an easy tone. He recognized the embarrassment on Gerard's face —he'd seen it more than once on a recruit who'd screwed up badly enough to lose a position.

Gerard nodded.

"And you've been off the drink?" Marcus guessed.

Gerard nodded again.

"I'm sure Bette will be glad to hear it," Bastian said. "But we're not here for that."

Gerard's expression brightened. "You're here about the beast! I *knew* you'd come."

"You knew?" Julianne pressed.

Gerard nodded. "Beast that big can't vanish forever. I knew it'd be back, and when it was, you'd come looking for me."

Bastian leaned forwards. "How can you be so sure you saw anything?" He left the last part off—how could Gerard be sure of anything *if he'd been steaming drunk?*

"I know what you think." Gerard leaned back, hooking his fingers in his belt. "I know I did wrong, but I wasn't drunk! Even I wouldn't stoop so low."

"You… weren't?" Marcus asked skeptically.

Gerard shook his head. "Oh, I smelled like I was. And yeah, I was late for my shift, and after I saw the bastard creature I was too busy pissing myself to talk sense—but I wasn't drunk!"

"Why wouldn't you tell Bette that?" Suspicion creased Marcus's brow into a frown.

Gerard shrugged. "I wasn't drunk, but I was hungover. Not much better, is it?"

Julianne narrowed her eyes. "There's an easier way to go about this." She held up her hands towards Gerard's face, expecting him to pull away.

Instead, his eyes lit up. "You'll read my memory?"

Julianne nodded. "With your permission."

She didn't need the physical contact, but over her many years as a mystic, she'd found people accepted her magic easier if they didn't have to think about how easy it was for her to slip into their minds from a distance. Julianne's eyes glowed softly.

Marcus watched, arms folded. Though his first instincts told him Gerard was lying, something didn't sit right. The man was too eager to let the mystic investigate him, and besides, this was Gerard—Marcus knew he drank like a fish, but he'd never seen him turn up to patrol drunk.

Julianne's eyebrows shot up, and she gasped in surprise. Then, grinning, she turned to Marcus and Bastian. "He spilled rum on his shirt and forgot to wash it. He wasn't drunk... a little hungover, but not drunk."

Her face fell slack again, and she probed further. Marcus tracked the set of her face—smooth and young, and trained to hide emotion, she still read like an open book to him.

There it was—the barest twitch of a brow, and the tiniest pull to one corner of her mouth. Julianne was worried. A brief, shallow flicker of her jaw made Marcus's heart speed up. She was *really* worried.

"What is it?" he asked a bare moment before her eyes cleared.

"Gerard did see something," she said quietly.

She waved her hands and whispered. An image appeared in the middle of the room. It was Gerard, watching the rift. Soft rain made the image hazy.

He was distracted, pacing and looking towards the trees. Twice, he stopped and placed a hand on his stomach.

"The others were patrolling for remnant," Julianne explained softly. "Three burst into camp. Gerard was supposed to go with them, but his hangover was making him feel ill. He bribed Lewis to swap stations."

Gerard—the real one—nodded. "If I'd sucked it up and gone

145

out, Lewis would've been the one to see the beast. They'd have believed him."

Julianne touched his arm. "What's passed has passed. All you can do is learn from it."

Marcus jabbed a finger at the still-moving illusion. "Look, something's coming through."

Image-Gerard had turned to rest his head against a tree trunk. The rift flickered and swelled, edges puffing out and twisting into impossible shapes.

The weapon came out first. A sharp, jagged blade, wickedly curved and shimmering like finely polished glass.

The beast that followed was more man than animal. Oddly proportioned and clad head to toe in armor, it shoved through the pulsing doorway and tumbled from the rift, landing on hands and knees in the mud.

Gerard watched, awe-struck as the invader stood on two feet and turned back to the rift. It reached in, then heaved back, pulling something with it.

A terrified Gerard scurried back into the trees, then fled. The image dissolved.

"How?" Gerard whispered. "I didn't see all that. I was too scared, too hungover."

"You saw it," Julianne said. "But terror and a healthy respect for your sanity made you forget the details, blurred out the worst parts."

Tears shined in Gerard's eyes. "I knew I wasn't crazy. But I swear on the honor of the Queen Bitch herself, I'm never going to touch a drop of alcohol again."

Bastian cleared his throat. "This is bad, Master Julianne."

Marcus nodded. "It's world-ending. If Gerard gives up drinking, who am I going to spend my nights with?"

Julianne thwacked his arm, and he winced. "Gerard, you're doing the right thing, and if anyone—" she darted a glance at Marcus "—fucks this up for you, I'll rain fire on them."

Gerard swallowed and nodded. His awed expression suggested he was just a little afraid that fire might rain on *him* if he fucked it up himself.

"As to that?" She waved a hand at where her illusion had stood moments before. "We need to close the portal and hunt down that alien creature, and whatever it brought through with it."

"Sure," Bastian said skeptically. "We'll just shut it. No big deal. It's only a doorway formed by impossible technology and powered by Bitch-knows-what, manned by giant clobbering monsters who want us all dead…"

Julianne grinned. "Sounds fun, doesn't it?"

Marcus chuckled. "This is going to be a blast."

CHAPTER TWENTY-ONE

"I appreciate you both coming to warn me," Annie said. "I just wish there were something I could do to help." She patted Ardie, who was nestled in a small bowl full of paper scraps on the table.

"You're more than welcome, Annie," Danil said. "But are you sure you won't move in closer to town for a bit?"

Annie darted a glance to the window, then wiped her hands nervously on her apron.

Julianne eyed the apron curiously. Something very unusual was going on.

"Annie," she asked. "Are those *frills* on your apron?" She didn't mention the lacy trim on Annie's dress.

Annie coughed, cheeks pink. "And what if they are? A woman's allowed to have a frill here and there if she wants."

Danil looked bewildered, then startled when he realized Julianne was blocking her thoughts from him.

"Your curtains are new, too," Julianne commented. She darted a look at Danil, then slipped a thought in his mind. *Don't interfere. This is girls' business.*

Danil slunk down in his seat, sighing. He knew he wouldn't get a word in edgewise in this conversation.

"And," Julianne continued, "I noticed that your herb bed has a few flowers ready to pick."

Annie was known for her uncanny ability to grow things, but her garden was usually as practical as the woman herself—nourishing foods, medicinal herbs, and the occasional culinary spice grew all through her gardens, but never had Julianne seen bright flowers sprouting up from freshly turned beds.

Annie turned around and stomped away without a word. A corner of Julianne's mouth turned up, quickly stifled as the old woman returned, untied her apron, and sat.

"Fine. I should have figured on you working it out." Annie stopped and chewed the inside of her lip.

Seeing she was struggling to open the conversation, Julianne reached over to touch Annie's hand. "I'm very happy for you," she said.

Annie's eyes popped open, and she scowled. "I thought you'd have more manners than to read a mind uninvited, young lady!"

Julianne laughed. "Oh, Annie. I didn't read anything—come on, dressing up? Planting flowers, prettying up your house? There *has* to be a man involved."

"A what?" Danil yelped, jolting upright.

Annie's scowl persisted a moment, then softened into a girlish smile. "I suppose you're right. Cavill *does* like it when I wear the gifts he brings."

"Cavill?" Julianne prodded, leaning closer with a conspiratorial grin.

Annie nodded. "He's a trader. Came out this way because he heard I have the only white peppers in the region."

She stood, wandering over to the window. "He started coming by every few weeks, sometimes for spices, but then because he'd found a little lace trim, or a pretty bow he thought I'd like."

When she turned back to Julianne, her eyes glowed. "Damned man should know he doesn't need to spoil a leathery old bird like me!"

Danil opened his mouth but shut it when a boot connected with his shin under the table.

"And *you* should know you thoroughly deserve it," Julianne told her. "Has he met Francis and Harlon?"

Annie's face fell. "He has, but they don't know he's been visiting me. I'd planned to tell them, but all this business about portals and monsters... I just haven't had the time."

"And you're nervous, too," Danil pointed out, ignoring Julianne's warning glare.

Annie shook her head in protest, then sighed. "Alright, fine. I might be a little reluctant. Those boys loved their father, though it's been long enough since he died."

"Annie, I'm sure they'll want you to be happy!" Julianne stood and went to Annie, wrapping her arms around her and squeezing happily. "And so do I. Do I get to meet this special man?"

Annie grinned happily. "He's on his way right now! He's due to arrive in Tahn in the morning."

Julianne's joy turned to a sudden spark of fear. Annie saw her reaction and her face fell. "You don't think the traders will have trouble, do you?"

Julianne pursed her lips. "Whatever Gerard saw, it was a good week ago now. It hasn't attacked anyone, that we know of." Bastian's remarks about the damage to the school came back to her. "Not intentionally, anyway."

Annie turned back to the window. "I keep telling him, just settle in one spot. It's too damned dangerous to be traveling the roads while the world is all upended."

"That doesn't sound like you, Annie." Danil commented. "You're not one to run from danger."

Julianne sat down again, and Ardie wiggled in his bowl. He awkwardly tipped it up, tumbled out, and scurried over to her. She cupped her hands, and he burrowed into them, tickling her with his tiny paws and dangling snout.

Annie shook her head. "I lost one man to a stupid accident. I don't plan to lose another that way."

"I'll send an escort out first thing," Julianne said. "We'll make sure he gets here safe. He might have to stay a while, though. I'm going to suggest to Francis and George that we close the roads—just temporarily."

Annie nodded. "I knew you had your head screwed on, girl. And I appreciate you looking after my man."

Julianne lifted Ardie. "While we're here, Annie, do you mind if we do some work?"

Annie eyed her. "Why would you come all this way to play a few magic tricks?"

"Yes, Julianne," Danil asked pointedly. "Why *would* you?"

Julianne bit her lip, then decided she couldn't lie to Annie. "Because the others would have a blue fit if they knew what I was doing. It has to be done, though."

"And I suppose I'm here to pull you out by the scruff of the neck if things go wrong?" Danil asked, voice loaded with resignation.

"Well I can't exactly ask Bastian to do it, he's exhausted!" Julianne nestled Ardie in her lap.

"And Marcus?" Danil asked. "You said you'd talk to him about it first."

Julianne shrugged. "I'll tell him later. Come on—are you willing to help? If not, you can go back to town, and I'll do it myself."

Danil barked a laugh. "Have you ever known me to run from a conspiracy?"

Annie cleared her throat. "Is what you're doing dangerous?" she asked.

"Definitely," Julianne said, looking her in the eye.

"And will it save lives?" Annie pressed.

"If I can pull it off? It might bring an end to the portal, and the monsters coming through it." She patted the little critter in her hands. "Not you, Ardie. Just the mean ones."

Annie sighed. "Fine. But I'm not lying for you!"

"You won't need to," Julianne said with a grin.

"Well, you two do what you need to—but stay out of my way, I have a kitchen to scrub today and then I need to air out my rugs." Annie eyed them, hands on hips. "And thank you. I do enjoy the visits, even when you're up to something… Which, I guess, is always."

She stalked out of the room, and Danil sighed. "You're going to do something really stupid, like try and form a mind-link with a non-human creature, aren't you?"

Julianne nodded.

"And there's no way I can talk you out of it, is there?" he asked.

She shook her head.

"Well, then, let's get on with it."

He blew out a long breath, and his face relaxed. Julianne felt his mind brush gently against hers—not enough to form a solid connection, but he would know if she was in trouble.

Julianne took a few breaths of her own, closing her eyes to find her center. She acknowledged the flutter of nerves in her stomach. She would be an idiot not to be afraid, but it didn't mean she would let the fear control her.

She opened her eyes and lifted Ardie so she could look into his beady little eyes.

"Will you let me in, little one?" she crooned. Then, her eyes misted over.

Julianne reached towards the creature in her hands. Ardie curled into a ball but didn't click his armored carapace shut. That was an improvement.

Ever since Bastian had mentioned the possibility of linking with the creatures, she'd made sure to use her magic around

Ardie, letting him grow accustomed to it. Julianne slipped a scrap of paper from a pouch at her belt and offered it to Ardie.

He sniffed and unfurled a little. As he reached for the snack, she pushed her spell towards him.

He accepted the brush of her mind without flinching. Julianne narrowed her focus and slipped into his mind.

It was like nothing she'd ever experienced before. Sensations and images flooded her mind, pressing in on all sides, constricting and wrapping her in a new reality.

This was something else. The random, animalistic thought patterns that saturated her came with a vague familiarity. It brought to mind her contact with the remnant.

Where the remnant had been vicious and violent, though, Ardie's mind was more sedate. Hunger, and the tantalizing scent of processed wood filled her nostrils and warm joy filled her belly as Ardie snatched the paper from her distracted fingers.

The sense of claustrophobia eased as Ardie ate. With a start, she realized the tightness was caused by his shell and eating made it soft and pliable for a brief period of time.

Feeling as though she was beginning to find her feet, Julianne tried something else. She formed a mental image of the rift and gently pushed it to Ardie.

The feeling of tightness snapped back, not as a physical manifestation but in the form of a memory. Frantic panic washed over her as she felt the ground pull away below. Her legs pulled in, and her head snapped down into a tight, protective ball.

She was shoved at the rift, pushed through and held in the suffocating bowels of a tight, pulsing tunnel.

The air grew stale. Julianne heaved a breath, and, when her lungs could stand it no more, she flicked back out of her hard shell and scrabbled for air. Something hard blocked her retreat, so she pushed forwards instead.

It was like trying to shove through a tight tunnel of pillows underwater. Every movement was a struggle against the sludge-like resistance, and the tiny pockets of air weren't enough to satiate her straining lungs.

Julianne forced her mind to stay with Ardie, to relive the memory of his trip through the portal. She felt his agony and desperation as he clawed his way through, searching for freedom, for a breath of precious air.

Finally, as dark spots clouded her vision and her limbs grew weak, the scent of fresh rain leaked through. A new surge of energy sent her scrambling, pushing, shoving through the suffocating portal.

A clawed hand reached forwards, latching into something solid. She pulled it back, then jerked in fright as she realized it was another vark—this one hadn't made it to freedom.

The spike of fear chewed through her energy but created a drive of its own. With a heave and a grunt, her long snout finally forced through the oppressive walls and sucked in a deep, giddy breath.

Julianne felt something release from her mind. For a moment, panic rose in her throat. Was someone in her head?

No, she realized. Something was in *Ardie's* head. She hadn't noticed the other consciousness at first, overwhelmed by the unfamiliar sensations and thoughts.

She pulled back her magic and took a steadying breath.

"You good there, Jules?" Danil asked.

She nodded, then released the spell. Julianne looked down at the tiny creature in her hands, still feeling a residual tinge of grief at the loss of one of its brethren.

"You poor thing," she crooned. "Shoved into that Bitch-damned portal and dumped in a strange world, all alone." She rubbed Ardie's head, and he nuzzled it sadly, then clawed his way up her sleeve to sit on her shoulder.

"You're pale," Danil pointed out.

She nodded. "I'm exhausted. But… I think I have what I need."

"You know how to stop Gerard's new friend?" Danil queried.

Julianne shook her head. "No. I don't think Ardie will be able to tell me that. I can connect with him, but he's still more animal than person, in the way he thinks. The portal on the other hand…"

The feel of gasping for breath, and the vark that hadn't made it had given her an idea. *I just need to nail down the details*, she thought, before planting her hands firmly on the table and standing.

Julianne stood and felt Ardie's momentary shift in balance as she moved. She froze.

"What is it?" Danil asked, grabbing her arm.

Julianne's eyes widened as she carefully probed the edges of her own mind, careful not to embrace her magic to do so.

"Danil… I can still feel Ardie."

"You mean you can't release the spell?" Danil asked, face drawing in to a worried expression.

"Annie?" Julianne called.

The old woman bustled in, alerted by the edge to Julianne's tone.

"What's wrong?" She looked from Julianne to Danil, then to the little vark on Julianne's shoulder.

"Annie, what color are my eyes?"

"Blue," Annie said, just as Danil yelped.

"They're clear!" he said. "Are you still—"

"Yes!" Excitement laced Julianne's voice. "I'm not casting a spell, or stuck in one, I'm sure of it! But I can feel him, Danil."

"Feel what, now?" Annie asked, frowning.

"I've made a permanent connection with Ardie," Julianne gushed. "That's… Well, it's never been done before, that's for sure!"

"I don't think that's exactly what happened," Danil said slowly. His eyes were locked on Annie's, but Julianne knew he'd be using the old woman's vision as his own.

Annie's eyes were riveted on Julianne… but not on her face.

"It's Ardie," Danil said in awe. "I... think he's using magic. Look at his eyes!"

Julianne carefully lifted the vark, detaching his claws from her shirt. "What are you up to, little guy?" she asked, eyeing his glowing red eyes.

Ardie snuffled his snout towards her, and she felt his desire to cuddle. She cradled him close, and wondered what, exactly, she'd gotten herself into.

CHAPTER TWENTY-TWO

"Goodbye, Annie!" Julianne hugged her friend. "I'll send word as soon as the escort for Cavill is organized.

"Thank you, my girl," Annie said. She grabbed Danil's arm. "You can't go without something for the journey, though."

"We rode," Danil laughed. "You're only twenty minutes out of town."

Still, he let her drag him back to the kitchen and load his arms with a warm, wrapped package that smelled of fresh biscuits.

"I know what young men are like. Always running around, forgetting to eat. And that Master of yours—you make sure she gets some of these, now!" Annie patted the bundle.

"Thanks, Annie," Danil said and gave her a peck on the cheek.

"Danil?" Julianne called.

"Yeah?"

"Where are the horses?" Julianne's voice was laced with worry.

He sighed. "Mathias *swore* they were trained not to run off." He vacantly looked along the dirt road that led from the Madlands to Tahn.

Julianne glanced at him and screamed. "Danil!" She flung a hand up, pointing at the roof.

Danil reeled, his magic showing him what she saw.

Two remnant leapt off Annie's roof, landing easily and circling around Danil and Julianne. Their nasty grins exposed broken teeth and their lank hair clung to sweaty faces in the mid-morning sun.

"Horse tasted good," one growled.

"You'll taste better," the other one hooted, then plunged forwards.

"No!" Danil screamed as a remnant body slammed him. His arm, still clutched around the little parcel, crunched against his chest. "Not the biscuits! You'll die for that, you stinking Bitch-forsaken monster!"

He twisted and ducked, barely avoiding a blow from a gnarled fist. Dropping the biscuits to the ground and kicking them to the side, Danil dropped into a crouch.

He cursed. Julianne was facing off with two of the beasts. *Typical*, he thought. *Pick on the girl. Pity—for you—she's not the easy target here.*

Annie was still inside, running for the kitchen. *Good, stay in there where it's safe.* Danil didn't have a set of eyes to 'borrow', but his training with Polly had taught him he didn't need to see in order to hit a target.

Danil breathed out slowly, focusing his senses on his immediate surroundings. He identified the sounds of Julianne's fight, then blocked it out.

"Stupid human," the remnant spat. "I'll eat your shiny eyes first."

Danil kicked towards the sound, and his foot connected. Bones crunched, and the remnant stumbled back.

He didn't give it a chance to move, instead rushing in and dropping to the ground, elbow first.

His aim wasn't quite true. Instead of soft belly, his elbow

smashed into hard bone. He yelped in pain but rolled off before the remnant could kick him in the face. A rush of air past his cheek suggested he was only *just* fast enough.

Now on his back, Danil paused a moment. His position was bad, but standing to face the wrong direction would be worse.

The crunch of footsteps on dirt gave away his enemy's position. Danil waited until he heard it again, then grabbed with both hands.

He latched onto the boot near his head and yanked. The remnant toppled and scrambled away while Danil jumped to his feet.

"Fight!" the remnant screamed. "Stop playing and fight!"

"If you say so," Danil muttered. He ran forwards, ducked, and snapped the edge of his hand into the remnant's throat. A high kick planted against its face, a satisfyingly wet crunch letting Danil know that this time, his aim had been true.

A gargled shriek let Danil know where to aim his final blow. This time, his kick was followed by the thump of a body against the ground. One more stomp with his heel silenced the beast.

Danil flicked his magic towards Julianne, using her eyes to see what she was up against. She'd taken out one of her attackers, but a blow to the ribs had winded her. She clutched one hand to her side, Ardie nestled in the bend of her elbow.

Julianne ducked a swing, grunting in pain. The remnant slammed into her, sending her spiraling on the ground.

The remnant stood over her, cackling.

Julianne smiled back. "Goodnight," she said.

A hollow ding rang out, and the remnant's eyes opened wide as it crumpled to the ground. Annie stepped back and lowered the skillet.

"Let me guess," she said. "Left all your weapons on the horses?"

Julianne nodded guiltily. "I didn't think even a remnant was dumb enough to start a fight in *your* yard," she said.

"Well," Annie said. "They won't be doing it again." Her face wrinkled in thought. "You've got a point, though. Even as close as I am to the Mads, there hasn't been a remnant brave enough to show its face here since... Well, since I was a young girl."

"Something has them restless," Julianne said. She toed the remnant with her boot, and it stirred. "And I think it's about time we ask them what's going on."

Danil groaned. "You're not..." he asked, then heaved a weary sigh when Julianne slipped her hands under the remnant's arms.

"Annie, do you have some rope?" she asked.

"Sure do," Annie replied, vanishing into the house.

"I'll be out in the barn!" Julianne called, then began dragging the unconscious remnant.

For a moment, Danil stood watching the twin trails the remnant's boots left in the dirt. Then, he walked over and grabbed the beast's ankles. "Marcus is going to kill me," he griped. "He warned me. 'Don't let her do anything stupid', he said. Did I listen? *Nooo*, not Danil. I *trusted* my 'wise and responsible' leader."

"Good thing you did," Julianne said happily, dropping the body with a dusty thump. "Or we wouldn't have the chance to get to the bottom of this."

"I don't even know what we're getting to the bottom of!" Danil protested, still holding the remnant up by its travel-worn boots.

Julianne dragged a stool over, then stood on it. "Over here, Annie," she called a moment before the old lady popped her head in.

"If you're planning to gut the thing, I'd appreciate it if you move the leathers out of the way," Annie said dryly.

She waved at a saddle sitting near some strung-up bridles and bits.

Danil dropped the feet and winced as a booted heel landed on his toe. "I'll do it," he said. He grabbed the heavy saddle and lumbered outside to drop it on the grass.

Annie helped him gather the smaller parts. By the time the riding gear was safely outside, Julianne had tied one end of the rope to her captive's wrists and ankles and flung the other over a tall beam.

She leaned backwards, using her weight to lift the remnant, feet first, into the air.

"Hand?" she gasped, cheeks red with the effort.

Danil darted over to help her. "What's this guy been eating?" he asked. The remnant's head and shoulders finally lifted off the ground to leave it swinging gently from the rafters.

Either the soft movement, or the surge of blood rushing towards the floor woke it up. It struggled and snapped but couldn't slip from the tight bonds.

"He might weigh more than Mack after a good feed, but he's a bit thin," Julianne calmly commented.

Danil nodded. Through Julianne's eyes, he could see the shadows in the remnants cheeks and the hollow dips near its collarbones. "Must be slim pickings out there, when all you have to eat is the odd rabbit," he agreed. Then, Danil's lips twitched into a smile. "Mmm, I could go for a bit of juicy rabbit." He licked his lips and rubbed his stomach.

The remnant writhed and grunted.

"Or a leg of lamb," Julianne said. "Remember what Mary served us up the other night? It was so rare, and the blood made a big pool underneath it."

"I'll eat *YOU*!" the remnant screamed, the imagery becoming too much for it. It kicked and bucked, desperate to escape.

"No," Julianne said. "You'll hang here and starve. Not a fast death, and not a quiet one. Not unless you tell me what I need to know."

"Then you'll feed me?" the remnant asked, eyes lighting up.

Danil snorted. "Sure. We'll set you free to ravage our countryside and kill our friends."

The remnant nodded eagerly, ready to make the deal.

Julianne groaned while Danil laughed. "You're even dumber than the usual meatheads we get around here, aren't you?" he asked. "No, moron. We're not going to set you free."

The remnant howled, then bared its teeth. "I ain't telling you nothing. Eat me!"

"I'd rather eat this," Danil said, pulling out a small bread roll and biting into it. "Mmm. Delicious!" He tore off another chunk with his teeth.

Behind the remnant, Julianne screwed up her face and shook her head. *Where did you get that?* she sent.

Danil shrugged. *I was saving it for later!*

"Look, you big ugly monster," Julianne said, tweaking the rope so the remnant swung around to face her. "If you answer a few easy questions, I'll feed you. I'll kill you straight after, but I'll try to make it as painless as possible."

"And if I don't, you'll torture me?" It sneered.

Julianne shook her head. "I'll put a plate of freshly skinned rabbit on the floor, just out of reach. Then, we'll go. All of us. And we'll let you gnash your teeth and stare at that juicy rabbit until it goes rancid, and you die of hunger." She rested a hand on her hip. "Understand?"

The remnant let out a howling roar and writhed, swinging back and forth hard enough that Julianne had to jump out of its way.

She waited patiently for the beast to vent its rage and frustration. Finally, the remnant quieted.

"I want to know why the remnant are on the move," she asked.

The remnant growled, slowly turning in circles as the rope twisted.

"Are you running towards something, or away from it," Julianne asked.

The remnant stayed silent. It glared at her, rheumy, yellowed eyes moving from one side to the other as it turned. Once its back was to her again, Julianne called out. "Annie!"

A door slammed inside the house, and footsteps approached. Annie walked into the barn, holding a plate of dripping meat. Her hands were still bloodied from chopping it into rough portions

"Set it down there," Julianne told her, gesturing to a low shelf.

The coppery scent of blood filled the barn, souring the smell of fresh hay and old horse dung.

The remnant growled again, this time in a higher, more desperate pitch.

"I'll ask again," Julianne said patiently. "Why are the remnant traveling so far from their homes?"

It spat at her.

"You're fighting a lost cause, girl," Annie said. "You can't bargain with a rock."

Stifling a growl of her own, Julianne stood. "You're right. I should have known the stupid beast wouldn't cooperate. Shall we go?"

Danil joined her, and they headed for the door.

"I'll break free!" the remnant screamed. "I'll come for you, bitch! Kill me now, or I come for you!"

Julianne ignored it and pulled the door closed behind her.

"*WAIT!*" The screaming inside the barn rose to a shrill shriek. "WAIT! I TALK!"

Grinning at Danil, Julianne shoved the door back open.

"You get one chance," she said, lifting a finger. "One! Why are the remnant—"

"We're getting killed!" the remnant screamed. "The sky opened, and monsters poured out. They cut off our heads and trampled our bodies! We ran, and we still run, and we kill those we see, but then we run!"

It fell silent, breath heaving. Julianne slowly walked over to the plate of bloody meat and picked a slice up between her fingers. She flicked it at the remnant, who had to twist to one side to catch it between its teeth.

"You're lying," Danil said. "Monsters pouring through the rift?

Our people have only seen tiny little things, and only a few at that. Nothing that could take on a horde of remnant."

Julianne dangled a second piece of meat just out of the remnant's reach. It shrieked, the hoarse wail quickly fading to a groan.

"I told you what I saw. The cracks are bad! More bad than human scourge!"

"Cracks?" Julianne snapped. "There's more than one?"

The remnant froze. Then, a wicked smile spread across its face. "Food first."

Julianne considered, then flicked it a second bite. "Not another morsel until you tell me—how many rifts have you seen?"

It swallowed the scrap without chewing. "We ran from one. Thought we were safe, just human rabble to fight. Then we saw the other. Tiny, but it will grow. It will flood your land and all you be eaten by blood monsters." The remnant opened its mouth wide, waiting expectantly.

Julianne tossed another bit of meat, then another.

"You think he's telling the truth?" Danil asked, watching blood run from the remnant's mouth while it forced the meat down its throat, choked, then tried again. The food seemed to be having trouble fighting the forces of gravity.

"No reason for it to lie," Julianne said, her face worried. "And it matches what Hannah showed me."

"Well, then," Danil said. "What is it they say about a creek full of shit and no paddle?"

The remnant caught another toss of meat, this one a little bigger than the others. It snorted and chomped, then swallowed. The meat got stuck—the remnant's eyes bulged, and its mouth opened, gasping for air.

"Uhh, Jules?" Danil pointed to the suffocating beast. "Should we do something about that?"

"Oh, damn." Julianne walked over to the remnant. It struggled, trying to dislodge the food that obstructed its airway.

She reached into her pocket and with a swift strike, plunged a blade into its eye. The remnant bucked one more time, then fell still. "Come on," she said. "We'll need to bury this before we go. I don't want Annie to come back to a rotting bag of meat in her barn."

"Going?" Annie said. "Who said I'm going anywhere?"

Danil raised his eyes to the barn ceiling in frustration. Just because he couldn't see, didn't mean he couldn't eye-roll with the best of them.

"Annie, you're coming," Julianne said. There was an edge to her voice—not angry or frustrated, but the pure confidence of someone who has authority and respect. "The remnant are coming too close, and we can't spare the men to watch this far out."

Annie opened her mouth to protest, but Julianne added, "And you know the guard would refuse to leave you unprotected, even at the expense of the town."

Annie heaved a sigh. "Fine. I hate it when you talk sense, girl, but I'll come. Just let me pack some things."

CHAPTER TWENTY-THREE

"Just get it done!" Jessop barked at the men tidying up the destroyed worksite. "We're not out here to make it pretty!"

Bastian dropped the log he had dragged over to the pile and stretched his aching back. When Julianne had returned from Annie's the previous day, he'd wanted to head out to secure the building site immediately, but she'd convinced him to wait until morning.

Now, a blanket of unease had settled over the workers. They were pushing hard, lifting beams and posts that days before had taken twice the number of men to heave into place.

Jessop saw Bastian stop work and hurried over.

"We nearly done, Jessop?" Bastian asked.

Jessop nodded. "I just want to reinforce what's left of that wall over there. Don't want it coming down on someone's head when we return."

Bastian's eyes dropped to the ground. "You think we ever will?"

Jessop snorted. "You think you could stay away? I've seen the passion you have for this place, boy. You'd take out a beast the size of a mountain to get this school built and running."

A grin touched Bastian's lips. "Yeah. Yeah, I would. Let's hurry, though—as much as I want to come back and fix it all up, right now, this place is giving me the creeps."

Jessop let out a cry of encouragement to the men. "Hurry your asses, boys, and we'll be back in time for Mary's lunch special. She's got the ragu on today!"

A rumble of excitement went through the worksite and Bastian's own stomach grumbled appreciatively.

"Catch!" Mack called out.

Bastian swung around just in time to catch the broken post-end Mack tossed to him.

"How you holding up, brains?" Mack asked.

"Honestly?" Bastian grinned. "Sore as shit. I can't tell you how much I appreciate you guys coming to help out. This would have taken days otherwise!"

Mack laughed. "Thank Mary. She heard you boys were coming out this morning and promised anyone who joined you would get a free feed."

"I'd marry Mary if I wasn't taken," Bastian chuckled.

Something slapped the back of his head, sending him stumbling forwards.

"The only reason that wasn't followed by a kick to the balls is because it's Mary," Tansy snapped. Then, she stood back, arms folded. "Mind you, I'd marry her too. Have you *tasted* her ragu?"

Bastian rubbed his skull. "Yeah, I have. It's good enough to make up for a whack to the back of the head."

Tansy laughed, then took the lump of wood from Bastian's hands. She tossed it over her shoulder and, without looking, managed to land it right in the middle of the pile of smaller debris.

"Was that the first bit of rubbish you picked up?" Mack asked her.

Bastian winced. Tansy had busted her ass like the rest of them, and she wouldn't take the slight lightly.

Tansy walked up to Mack and stared up into his eyes.

"Or did you see other guys before Bastian?" Mack finished. Then, he burst into laughter.

"Fuck you," Bastian grumbled.

Tansy didn't respond. She was too busy giggling.

"*HALT*!" Jessop yelled.

Everyone froze, looking about warily. Those standing near the remaining upright structures glanced up, and some began shuffling away with worried looks.

Jessop grinned. "We're done. It's lunch time!" When people started ambling towards him, he barked again. "What, you think this is a trash can? Pick up your tools, you lazy bastards!"

"I'll go get our horses ready," Tansy said. She leaned in to give Bastian a peck on the cheek but stopped and drew away. "Oh, Bitch's ass. You're going for a bath before you eat, you smelly bastard."

She pranced away, Bastian watching in awe as she trotted happily toward the horses.

"You're so screwed," Mack said.

Bastian nodded. "That I am, friend. That I am."

Tansy smirked, overhearing his words, but didn't turn back. When she reached the horses, she finally let herself slump over and rub her eyes.

"Bitch's oath, that was a long day," she groaned. She leaned down to touch her toes, then rolled herself back up to a standing position and yawned wide enough to crack her jaw.

"Now, where did I hide that water?" She dug through her saddlebag and pulled out the leather waterskin with a grin.

She took a long pull, then splashed some carefully on her hands. She rubbed the dirt off her face, eyes closed.

A twig snapped.

"Took you long enough," Tansy said, using her shirt to wipe the muddied water from her face.

An uneasy feeling prickled along her spine, and she swung around. "Bast—"

Before her stood a man. Or, perhaps, not a man—but shaped like one, clad head to toe in heavy armor that shone red in the morning light.

"Oh... shit."

One hand reached out to her horse and grabbed the pommel of the saddle. The horse's flesh twitched and shivered as it stood, frozen in terror. She risked a quick glance back.

"Shiiiit!" she whimpered. Behind her stood a lumbering beast, red-skinned and covered in the same carapace the vark's wore. Only this was no vark...

Two long, spindly legs with jagged spikes held up a round, scaly body. Its head was squat, and the long vark-like snout stretched almost to the ground. Folds at the top opened and then flapped shut as the beast breathed heavily.

The man-monster said something unintelligible, and Tansy jerked her gaze back to him. She couldn't see his expression, hidden behind the closed visor.

She did see his raised hand and the quick gesture that ended in a thick finger jabbed towards her.

The beast behind her rustled. Tansy let her body move before her mind could process what she'd seen. She jumped, flinging herself up to a low branch just as the beast charged the spot she had stood in a moment before.

She swung, jumped to another branch, and then somersaulted into the ground. The monstrous man turned, his movements slowed by the heavy armor. He uttered a guttural call.

Tansy fled. She ran towards the worksite, unsure if she'd made a terrible decision and was leading the monsters to her friends—but she had to warn them.

The guard was there, or some of them, at least. They'd help.

"MACK!" she screamed as she burst into the clearing. "Monsters!" she gasped. "A big man, and he had a beast in the trees!"

Without taking a breath, the entire worksite sprang into action.

"Find weapons!" Jessop yelled as his workers scrambled for shovels, picks, crowbars—anything that would give them a fighting chance.

"Move back!" Mack barked. He moved towards the trail with Carey and Josh. "Gerard! You, too!" he snapped.

Gerard appeared from amongst the workers, face scared but posture resolute.

"You know how to fight this thing?" Mack snapped.

Gerard shook his head.

"Well, then I guess we're in this shit together." Mack grinned and tossed him a spear.

Gerard caught it. "Thank you. You can count on me, Mack."

Tansy stumbled over to Bastian.

"You ok?" he said.

She nodded and grinned. Then, she froze.

"Mack?" she squeaked. "Mack?"

Bastian turned to where Tansy was looking. "Oh, hell. MACK!"

Tansy's eyes locked on the beast she'd seen near the horses. How could it have gotten back there so fast?

More cries went up from another section of the clearing.

Bastian, eyes white, choked out a curse. "We're surrounded."

CHAPTER TWENTY-FOUR

"They're just ahead." Julianne's eyes cleared, and she stood high in her stirrups to see over the hump in the road.

In the far distance, a cloud of dust rose from the road. She knew it was Annie's trader friend. Cavill had, thankfully, heard of the mental magicians living in Tahn and hadn't been too terrified when Julianne had reached out to speak into his mind.

His initial shock had turned to relief at the approaching escort. He'd heard stories of the increasing remnant attacks and the strange little monsters that had arrived through a magical doorway in the forest.

Cavill's reaction was enough to let Julianne know any attempt at keeping a secret in the small, regional towns was futile.

"I can't wait to meet the lad!" Bette squealed. "To think, Annie with a man on her arm!"

Marcus rolled his eyes but stayed out of the conversation.

"He's more than a lad, lass," Garrett muttered. "If he's caught Annie's eye, he'll be older than the hills themselves!"

"A man in love is a lad at heart," Bette shot back.

"I'm all man, thank ye." Garrett stretched himself as tall as he could in his saddle and gave Bette a baleful glare when she laughed at him.

"Aye, yer all man, me love." Bette blew him a kiss.

"You know, you didn't *both* have to come," Julianne said. "It's just a trade escort."

"He's no trader—he's Annie's man!" Garrett said in surprise. "What do ye think she'd do to us if he came to grief on the road?"

"And what about Annie herself?" Bette snapped. "Always thinkin' about yerself, aren't ye?"

"It's me balls I'm thinkin' of," Garrett grumbled.

"They do seem to be on your mind a lot," Marcus said, finally joining the discussion.

"If Cavill is half as tough as Annie, he probably doesn't even need an escort," Julianne pointed out. "You're not here just to stickybeak, are you?"

Bette snorted, then coughed. "Who, me? Never."

Julianne just shook her head. "Well, don't say anything awful to him." Her eyes settled on Garrett as she said that.

He opened his eyes wide in feigned innocence. "Who, me? Never!"

Marcus laughed, then pointed ahead. "I can make them out. Not traveling very fast, are they?"

"Bloody Muirians think all the remnant strife is on our side of the road," Bette said. "When we've sent guards out to meet travelers, they take their sweet assed time gettin' to the halfway point, then run hell for leather to Tahn like a pack of wolves is on their back."

"Well," Julianne said. "They're right, aren't they?"

"Aye." Bette grinned. "But Tahn has us, so it's still a hundred times safer than anywhere else!"

She reached a hand out, palm facing Garrett. He slapped it in a proud high five.

Julianne's eyes flicked to the side of the road. The witchpost slid by, a stark and twisted reminder of how close danger really was.

"AHOY!" A cry from one of the trader's company reached her ears.

"Ho there!" Bette yelled back. "All well on the road?"

"Well enough." A grizzled guard trotted ahead of his group, making his way over to Bette.

When his horse reached hers, he stretched out a hand.

Bette grasped it in her own, giving it a solid shake. "Hello, Barnes." She'd met the hired escort before and had confidence in his ability to protect the traders he worked for.

"I hear things are getting a bit exciting down in Tahn," he said. "Want me to keep on with the journey, or pass over to you?"

"I'm sorry, Barnes," Cavill rode up to greet Bette with a polite nod. "This isn't a business trip—I really can't justify the expense of two escorts."

"Two?" Bette yelped.

"Cavill, we're not charging," Julianne gently explained.

Cavill looked uncomfortable at that. "You're not? I really can't accept that. You've come all this way, surely you'll let me—"

"And I wasn't offering to stay as a hire," Barnes broke in. "I've a mind to see this rift business myself. I'll plod along, no charge to you."

Pink flushed Cavill's cheeks. Curious, Julianne brushed against his mind. The trader really did feel bad about accepting services he hadn't paid for.

His strong moral code touched Julianne. She smiled at him. "Honestly, Cavill, it's no bother."

"Ah." Cavill looked around and motioned for the rest of his small company to catch up. Two women—one middle aged, one young—and a man who looked to be in his early twenties nudged their horses up to join him. "This is my family. We are all very grateful for your help."

The older woman came forward. "I'm guessing none of you

are Annie?" she said with a grin. "I can't wait to meet her. Pa has been a whole new person since they met."

"Hush, Dora." Cavill blushed again, but Dora just laughed it off.

"I hope she's not as stodgy as you, Pa. Come on. Let's go." She looked around expectantly, and Bette nodded.

"Aye, let's be off." She waved and kicked her horse, leading the way back to Tahn.

"So, you're the mystic queen?" Dora asked, falling in with Julianne.

"Master—I'm far from a queen," Julianne said.

Dora nodded thoughtfully. "And you're friends with Annie."

Julianne nodded. "I am. We all are."

Dora glanced at Julianne nervously. "This feels like a stupid question, but… she *is* nice, isn't she?"

"You haven't met?" Julianne asked. When Dora shook her head, Julianne understood why the woman seemed skittish. "She's old. A tough, leathery old woman who could strip your skin off with a few words."

She waited until that settled over Dora—who, surprisingly, didn't look at all upset by the description.

"But she's fiercely loyal, extremely kind, and very protective of those she loves," Julianne finished.

Dora sighed happily. "That sounds like the woman Pa talked about. Strange—she sounds the exact opposite of Ma, except the kind and loyal part. Ma was as timid as a dormouse. I don't know how she and Pa ever got anything done between them!"

"Sometimes, love comes from surprising places," Julianne said, glad Dora seemed taken by the thought of her father seeing someone as tough as Annie could be.

"I think it's just what he needs," Dora said. "And he must have fallen hard—the stories about forest monsters and remnant hordes would have him hiding under the bed any other time.

Look at him!" She pointed to her father who rode at the front of the group alongside Bette. "He's not even scared!"

Perhaps he should be, Julianne thought. She kept that to herself, but when she looked up, Marcus gave her a knowing glance. He'd been listening in and had the same thought Julianne had.

Keep your ears open, Julianne sent to him. *The lack of remnant about today has me more worried than relieved.*

Marcus gave a tiny nod to show he'd heard, then took up conversation with the boy who'd traveled with Cavill and Dora.

"Who's that?" Julianne asked.

"My son-in-law," Dora said. "Or, he will be if Amity gets her way."

"Ah." The young couple exchanged an infatuated glance as Julianne watched. "They seem happy together."

Dora rolled her eyes and groaned. "It's like living in one of those goopy tavern songs. Bitch help me if Pa and his new lady go all soppy like that."

Julianne couldn't hold back a giggle. "I promise, Annie is anything but soppy."

Dora raised a hand to her chest. "Well, thank goodness for that. I'd need a bucket otherwise."

They travelled on, but Julianne struggled to focus on the light conversation. Her mind kept pulling back to the road, and the eerie silence that followed the travelers.

"And then, Amity told him to—"

"Birds." Julianne's sudden thought cut off Dora's story. "There aren't any birds today."

Dora fell silent, immediately alert. Marcus reeled his horse back to Julianne, feeling her sudden spike of worry.

"Marcus, I haven't heard a single bird since we left the—"

A scream echoed through her mind, shoved into her consciousness by brute force.

Attack!

Bastian's terrified warning came with a barrage of images. A monstrous man clad in red armor. A cluster of guards and workers, herded into a group in the middle of a clearing. Three lumbering beasts with razor sharp claws and wickedly fast legs trapping them.

Julianne shoved the message at Marcus, Bette, and Garrett.

Fear soaked the air, and the horses shuddered and flinched, dancing in place as their owners strived to calm them.

"Garrett, Barnes—get Cavill and his people to Tahn and barricade the town. Bette, Marcus…"

"Julianne, you can't!" Marcus yanked on his reins to swing his horse around. "Go with Cavill. We'll take care of it."

"The hell you will," Julianne said. "I'm not missing this for anything!"

She shoved a burst of compulsion at the trader and his family. As one, they kicked their horses and raced for Tahn, Garrett and Barnes beside them.

Marcus stared at Julianne. "Last chance to bail," he said.

"Ha!" She kicked her horse towards the witchpost.

We're coming, she sent to Bastian.

CHAPTER TWENTY-FIVE

Polly rested a hand on Danil's face. He leaned in for a deep kiss.

Polly yelped. "You prick! What did you do that for?" She touched her lip where he'd bitten it.

"Sorry," he said, hoarse. His eyes darted left and right, then widened.

Polly jerked back. "What's wrong?" she asked.

Danil shot to his feet and started pulling on his clothes. Polly quickly grabbed her shirt and yanked it over her head.

"The worksite was attacked," Danil said. "It's... bad."

Polly's stomach flipped over. "And we're riding right into the thick of it?" she asked.

He paused. "Unless I can talk you into staying?"

"As if." Polly stepped into her boots without bothering to lace them. "Your socks are there." She let her eyes linger on the socks strewn on the table long enough for Danil to get his bearings, then ran outside.

"Tessa!" she cried. "I need your horses!"

Tessa stuck her head out the window next door. "What for?"

"Emergency," Polly said grimly. She vaulted over the fence and ran to Tessa's stable.

She hefted a saddle over one of the horses and pulled the straps tight.

"Here," Tessa said, running in and grabbing another saddle.

"No time," Polly said. "I'll go bareback."

"You ride better that way anyway." Tessa slipped a bridle onto the second horse while Polly tended to the one Danil would take. "Be careful. Send word when you're safe."

"I'll try," Polly said.

The stark fear on Danil's face was like nothing she'd ever seen, and she'd bet her ass that all three mystics would be racing for the same spot. Any messages back to Tahn would have to be taken by hand.

"Tessa…" Polly grabbed the older woman's hand. "I don't know what's going on, but Danil is scared out of his mind. I can't tell you what to prepare for…"

Tessa gripped Polly's shoulder. "We'll prepare anyway. Don't you worry about us, we're Tahn. We've got this."

Polly nodded as Tessa swung back the gate. As soon as the horses were outside, Polly vaulted onto the shorter one. "Come on, Danil!" she yelled.

He ran out of their cottage, stumbling over the doorstep. He straightened, then headed for his horse. He swung up without difficulty and grinned. "This is gonna be the craziest thing we've ever done."

"And what is that, exactly?" Polly asked.

"I'll explain on the way!" He kicked his horse and ran for the gates leading out of Tahn.

"Close the gates!" Danil yelled on the way through, then pulled his horse to a stop.

"Don't close them!" Polly yelled, seeing the small group of riders racing for safety. "Garrett's coming!"

The six riders dashed towards Tahn, only pulling their horses up once inside. Garrett kicked his in the ribs and trotted out again.

"Bitch-damned ass of a trick!" he swore. "Use that bloody magic on me, why I oughta—"

"Garrett!" Danil snapped. "Where's Julianne?"

Garrett looked crestfallen. "Off to have fun without me. Even Bette got to go!"

"You brought these guys in?" Polly asked. Garrett nodded, and she shrugged. "Then come out with us. Sounds like they can use all the help they can get."

Garrett brightened, then his face hardened. "Nah. Whatever's got yer master scared is a bad one. There's no tellin' who'll come out on top, and if ye lose out there…" He cast a glance over his shoulder at Tahn.

The streets were crowded with people who'd heard Polly and Danil's frantic race through town and seen the terrified travelers race inside the gates. Curiosity warred with fear on their faces and a nervous hum vibrated in the air as they muttered.

"Good man," Danil said. He grinned. "I'll try and save one for you."

"Yer a good lad!" Garrett called happily, and the couple turned to go. "Make sure it's a big'un!"

Bastian, we're coming, Danil sent, focusing his thoughts through the amphoral at his wrist. He still wasn't used to using the device, but damn if he wasn't glad he had it right now.

Hurry, Bastian sent back. *These bastards are—* he broke off, then resurfaced a moment later. *Are bastards.*

These bastards are bastards? Danil queried, pushing his horse along with another kick.

Fucking… bastards! Bastian's mind tried to knit back together. The shock of the attack and a blow to the head didn't make it any easier to string a thought together.

He risked diverting his attention to look around. Bodies littered the ground, but so did one of the large, long-nosed beasts. The guards and workers alike had fought valiantly, some to the death.

Now, what remained of them faced off against an impossible beast.

The armor-clad man had climbed atop one of the animals it had brought with it. Red metal shone beside the red carapace, and when the light hit them just right, it was like they'd melded into a single creature.

The second beast ducked and wove, snapping claws out at the weary humans. Between attacks, it followed the first, their movements so synchronized Bastian was sure it wasn't natural.

A growl came from one of them—probably the man, as the beast's mouth didn't open. It stalked closer, and the man drew a long, pointed weapon with a wicked curve to it.

We're here! The thought popped into Bastian's mind and relief made him sag. Just as hope seeped through him, his enemy screamed, thrusting its covered face towards him.

Bastian flinched, but grit his teeth and endured the loud shriek. He had felt Tansy's grip on his arm let go and knew she'd moved away.

The beast jerked and screamed, opening the small orifice under its snout to make the high-pitched sound. Bastian's ears ached, and his head throbbed.

The monster turned and bolted into the trees with its rider. A spear hummed past Bastian's ear, glanced over the retreating tail of the second creature, and clattered to the ground.

"Fuck," Mack whispered. "What in the ever-living fuck was that?"

Tansy stepped into Bastian's view. She held a spear of her own, this one tipped with dark, slimy blood. "I got it!" she crowed. "Right up the ass. It'll be shitting out of two holes for the rest of its very short life!"

"It's still out there," Bastian said quietly. He rubbed his head and tried to shake away the echoes of the piercing scream.

"That knock you took still bothering you?" Tansy asked, worried.

"Not the bump, the sound," he clarified.

"What sound?" Mack asked. He cocked his head to see if he could hear anything.

"My ears are still ringing, that's all. From its shriek?" he clarified when Mack and Tansy both looked bewildered.

"Bastian, we didn't hear a shriek," Tansy said. "It kind of hummed when I stabbed it, but it wasn't a shriek. I thought I'd missed until I saw the blood."

Hoofbeats erupted, and Bastian scrambled to his feet.

"It's gone," he told Julianne. "Ran off into the bushes. Two beasts left, and the… man-thing."

"One's injured?" Julianne asked. "I heard it scream." She shuddered at the memory.

Bastian raised his eyebrows to Tansy. "See! I don't know how you didn't hear it."

"Well, I didn't hear it either," Bette said. "No bloody clue what she was talkin' about. But I guess if ye heard it yerself, she didn't imagine it."

"It must have to do with mind-links," Julianne said. "Perhaps… the one we saw at the rift screamed so everyone could hear. Maybe this is a more evolved species. It must communicate telepathically."

"Well then, how did *he* hear it," Bette asked. She jabbed a hand behind her where Marcus was walking his horse into the clearing, hands clapped over his ears.

"He's a mystic, but he just won't admit it," Julianne said.

"Bullshit!" Marcus snapped. "I can block, but I don't have an ounce of magic in me."

"Then what do ye call blockin'?" Bette asked.

"Iron will," Marcus growled. He stuck a finger in his ear and wiggled it. "Next theory?"

"The monster's scream is a psychic defense," Julianne said. "We already know Ardie is sensitive around magic, and I mind-read him, so there's got to be—"

"You what?" Marcus screeched. "When?"

"Yesterday," Julianne said calmly.

"Yesterday? Who were you with—*DANIL*! I'm going to roast that bastard!"

"Please, I beg you, no," Danil said jovially behind them.

Marcus swung around, fists balled.

"Come on, man. Have you ever tried to stop Jules from doing something she was hell bent on?" Danil asked.

"*You* said it was dangerous!" Marcus said to Julianne. "Too dangerous for Bastian to try."

"It was," Julianne said. "But not so dangerous that it wasn't worth doing. Besides, Danil was there to pull me out if I needed it."

Marcus lifted his hands in the air, then dropped them to his sides. "Can't leave you alone for a day!" he muttered.

"Mmm," Julianne agreed. "You probably can't. I'm a bit of a troublemaker, aren't I?"

Bastian rubbed the back of his neck. "Sorry to interrupt, guys... but what the fuck are we going to do?"

"We need to shut down that Bitch-damned portal," Bette said. "Before that bastard pulls through another army of... whatever those things were."

"I think I know how to do it," Julianne said. "Jessop?"

The old man limped forwards. Blood dripped from a lump on his scalp, but his eyes were bright, and he seemed alert. "Yes, ma'am?"

"I need you to build us something," Julianne said. "But we need to do it in a hurry... and we need to build it at the rift. Get your men to bring whatever supplies they need. We leave now."

Jessop paled.

"Men!" Mack yelled. "You hear that? We're going to the rift, and we're going to stop these hellspawn coming through!"

A weak cheer rose through the crowd, and Mack shrugged

one shoulder up. "I tried. Gotta be honest, I'm not too excited about going back, either."

"It'll be fine," Julianne said. "What's the worst that can happen?"

They moved as one big group, carefully spreading out along the path towards the rift and staying as quiet as they could.

Bette was the first to step into the carnage.

"Oh, Lewis," she said. "Ye poor wee bastard."

Lewis's legs had been torn off his body and tossed on the ground. A few steps further, and she found the rest of the corpse.

The men looked to have put up a valiant fight. Bruises on arms and legs and faces showed they'd fought. Crushed hands and broken fingers suggested they'd fought hard.

Still, with only three men free to guard the portal while the rest of the crew had gone to make sure the workers were safe, they hadn't been able to fend off whatever attack they had faced.

"Did they come back here?" Mack asked, voice low and weapon high.

Julianne shook her head. "I don't think something came into the camp. I think something escaped from it."

She pointed at the ground, where thin, spiked prints marked the soft dirt.

"Two claws and long feet," Marcus said, bending down for a closer look. "But either this guy stayed around and danced the night away, or..." he trailed off.

"Or there was more than one," Bette said. "A whole damned lot more than one. And this isn't one of the wee beasties that knocked ye on yer ass," she pointed out.

Marcus coughed. "I wouldn't say I was on my ass, exactly."

"We have to get back to Tahn," Julianne said. "But not until we block off this portal."

"What if the bastards head to Tahn?" Marcus asked. "We can't leave the town undefended."

"If we don't shut down their access to our world, the fat

pricks will keep dragging their scaled asses over," Bette pointed out. "And if we don't have the men to fight the goat-fuckers off, we're fucked."

Julianne raised a hand. "Danil, you and Polly head back." She waved down Danil's protest. "We can't leave them undefended—at least if one of us is there, we can send out a cry for help if we need it."

Polly grabbed Danil's arm. "We'll go. We can help the town prepare, just in case. Right, dear?"

Danil nodded and the two of them ran off.

One by one, each of the crew of workers walked up and dropped their load by the rift. Some carried beams and heavy planks. Others had bags of clay and plaster, or packets of nails and belts full of tools.

Jessop already had his measuring stick out, checking the size of the beams and setting aside the ones he wanted.

The frame went up quickly. The boxed structure surrounded the portal, attached to a platform anchored to the ground by deep posts. Everyone helped to fill it. Globs of wet clay were layered between handfuls of rock and stone, buckets of wet adhesive filling any gaps between them.

They worked as fast as they could, but no amount of willpower could force each layer to dry faster. By the time the frame had been filled and the portal had vanished from sight, the shadows stretched long over the ground.

CHAPTER TWENTY-SIX

Danil trotted his horse along the road to Tahn. The poor beast had almost been run into the ground in the urgent race to the witchpost, and he didn't want to kill it, so he tempered their speed.

Polly leaned forwards. "Danil... Can you hear that?" She pulled her horse up and closed her eyes.

After Danil had insisted his hearing was better because he couldn't see, Polly had been practicing the trick. With her eyes closed, she really did feel like her other senses were heightened.

It didn't take supernatural hearing to pick out this noise, though. "Shit!"

"Polly, that sounds a whole like a giant horde of remnant. Tell me it isn't?" Danil's horse picked up on his anxiety and let out a high-pitched whine.

"Is it ahead or behind us?" Polly asked in a low voice, patting her own horse's neck to soothe it.

Dani shook his head. He pointed at the thick forest off to one side. "Both. Or, neither. They're headed right for us, and fast."

Polly could hear the rumble getting louder. Curses, yells, and the thwack of branches and leaves as the horde moved through it sent a shiver down her spine.

"Come on," she said. "We can outrun them."

They kicked their horses and ran, circling round a bend in the road. They shuddered to a stop, fear wrapping around their throats.

Stay. Very. Still. Danil sent the words to Polly with a thread of reassuring calm.

Polly couldn't have moved anyway. The sight of several hundred remnant rushing across the road into the trees on the other side had frozen her muscles and squeezed at her lungs.

A second horde, behind them, erupted from the dense foliage. They rushed at Polly and Danil, weapons raised. Danil flinched. There was no escape, the two groups had them hemmed in.

He sucked a breath and prepared to die. The remnant ran past, pushing and shoving and screaming.

Bodies pressed and shoved against the shuddering horses, and several of the remnant screamed insults and threats.

Danil felt the beast's eyes crawling over him, but whatever had them fleeing at that breakneck pace had such a grip, not a single one stopped to fight them.

The crowded press eased as fast as it had started. Remnant after remnant passed, then vanished into the trees across the road, leaving them suddenly alone.

Polly let out a sob, then slid off her horse and sat on the ground. Danil climbed down to join her, grabbing the reins of both horses so they couldn't run. He wrapped one arm around her shoulders.

"Sorry," she whimpered, trying to force down her shuddering gasps.

Danil squeezed her. "That," he said softly, "Was the scariest fucking thing I have ever encountered. Ever."

"You're n-not scared," she said, eyes still wet. Her voice was a little steadier, though.

"Are you fucking insane?" Danil asked. "Those bastards could have shoved us through a meat grinder backwards. Only an idiot wouldn't be scared." He winked. "I'm just really, really good at hiding it."

"Liar." Polly sniffled, then wiped her nose on his shirt.

Danil cupped a hand around her face. "I'm not kidding. I've spent my life at the Temple, learning to control my mind, master my emotions. I can hide fear; I can work through it and stay focused when I'm terrified. That doesn't mean I'm not shitting my pants."

"Teach me," she said, voice hard. "Teach me how to do that."

"Right now?" Danil asked, surprised.

Polly shook her head. "No. But soon." She took a deep breath. "If one of those bastards had taken a swing... I couldn't have moved if I'd wanted to. I couldn't have fought back."

Danil nodded slowly. "Ok. That's fair. You've taught me to fight with my eyes closed, I certainly owe you this." He rubbed her back. "But first, we have to get back to Tahn. I don't think those remnant are headed there, but I can't say I'm so sure about those things Bastian saw."

Polly nodded and stood on shaky legs. Danil helped her back onto her horse.

"You ok?" he asked, worried at how hard her hands trembled as she held the reins gripped in white fists.

Polly shook her head. Then, she grinned. "I'm scared as fuck. Not gonna stop me doing my job, though."

Danil couldn't stifle the wide smile that crept over his face. "That's my girl."

He mounted his horse, kicked its ribs, and they set off on the last leg of their journey.

When they arrived at Tahn, the sun had dropped low in the sky. Danil was relieved to see the gates firmly shut and lanterns dotting the top of the wall.

"Ahoy the gates!" Danil called as he dismounted. "It's your favorite mystic! Open up!"

A head poked over the wall. "Ye don't look like Julianne or Bastian," Garrett called. "In fact, ye look like that prick Danil—and he's nobody's favorite."

"Very funny, you vertically challenged little bastard." Danil waited, but the gates didn't open.

"If ye want to come in, I'd advise ye don't piss off the man who's holdin' the gate shut, ye smartassed wee prick." Garrett waited for a response.

"My prick is anything but small, little man. Now, open up." Danil smirked.

Garrett opened his mouth to shout something down, but Danil muttered something under his breath.

"Yes, Danil the great an' powerful. I shall bow at ye feet and lick yer dirty boots, for yer glory shines upon—"

"Danil, hurry the fuck up!" Polly snapped. "I'm cold and tired and some big fucking monsters are coming to kill us. Just get him to open the damn gate."

"Spoil all my fun," Danil grumbled. A moment later, the gate swung open and they rode in.

"You better hold that spell as long as you can," Polly suggested. "Because the second you let him out of it, he's going to hunt your ass down and give it a walloping."

Garrett gave them a limp wave, then closed the gate.

Danil winked at Polly. "Watch this." He waved a hand in front of Garrett, then placed a finger on the rearick's temple. "Garrett, you won't remember this. Instead, you think we traded insults for a while, then you opened the gate to let us in. You locked it after. But, you are now absolutely certain that my dick is bigger than—OW!"

Danil winced, rubbing the bruise forming where Polly had punched him. His finger had slipped off Garrett's head with the unexpected whack had interrupted his spell.

Garrett shook his head, dazed. Then, he slowly looked up.

"Why you little—" Garrett lunged.

Danil dropped his horse's reins and ran, taking off down the street. The furious rearick at his heels shouting in anger.

"Idiot," Polly murmured. She grabbed Danil's horse and led both animals back to Tessa's.

Her friend ran out to the road to greet her. "Is everything ok?" Tessa asked, voice breathy. "First you ran off, then Garrett came in and ordered the town locked up. He ran past just before, screaming at someone."

Polly giggled. "Yeah, that was Danil. I expect that to go on for a while."

Tessa put her hands on her hips. "Men! I swear, it's a wonder they get anything done in between dick measuring contests and —what's so funny?"

Polly had doubled over laughing at the words 'dick measuring contest'. She did her best to explain to Tessa that that was exactly why Garrett was trying to kill Danil.

By the time the two women had recovered from their laughter, a sore and sorry Danil had returned.

"What did he do to you?" Polly asked.

"I have a bruise on my ass an inch thick and a mile long." Danil rubbed his backside. "I think it broke the skin."

Polly sighed and shook her head. "You know what I'm going to say, don't you?"

Danil nodded sadly. "That I deserve everything I got? I had to use that spell, though! He wouldn't let us in, and who knows what could have followed us back!"

Polly snorted. "That's *not* the bit that I was complaining about, and you know it."

Danil sighed. "Look, you might have a point. I'm not admitting that you do, I'm just saying you might."

Polly walked past, head high. "Well, until I get a full apology, you'll just have to keep that big ol' dick of yours to yourself."

She slapped his ass, and he yelped in pain, but she ignored him. Tessa clapped a hand over her mouth but couldn't hold back a fresh round of giggles.

CHAPTER TWENTY-SEVEN

Marcus threw a glance over his shoulder. Above, trees loomed over them, obscuring the stars. Ahead, the long line of exhausted workers and guards marched towards home.

"I could fall asleep on my horse," Julianne murmured beside him.

Marcus nodded. "I know how you feel. Why don't you meditate for a bit? That'll recharge you a little, at least."

Julianne chewed her lip. "I don't feel safe diverting my attention," she said.

Marcus shook his head. "It's more dangerous for you to be so tired you can't stand up when the real fight breaks out."

Julianne sighed, then nodded. "Ok. We're only twenty minutes out. Will you take my horse?"

Marcus took the reins, holding them gently at his side. He was confident the horse would continue to amble along, while Julianne only spared the absolute minimum energy and concentration needed to not fall off.

They rode in silence, Julianne's eyes a soft white, Marcus's dark in the half-moon light. The men ahead spoke little, using quiet voices and constantly darting glances at the trees. Every sound brought a spike of anxiety, every stumbled step a jolt of worry.

The trees broke and finally, the walls of Tahn came into view. The bright, sparkling lanterns lifted the men's spirits, and they picked up pace, walking faster and talking a little louder.

Marcus heard a burst of quiet laughter. Another man started a loud joke. Then, a scream.

Bedlam broke out. Marcus's horse reared up, then charged ahead, ripping the second set of reins from his hand. Something crashed beside him and as he turned to look, the moonlight sparkled on a shiny surface, throwing hues of red and amber.

"Run!" Marcus screamed. "Run to Tahn!"

He wrestled with his horse as Julianne's bolted past, riderless. Terror turned his veins to ice as he jerked roughly, wheeling his horse around to face the terror.

The armor-clad monster stood in the pathway, sword raised menacingly. Behind it, a figure in white rested on the ground.

"*JULIANNE!*" Marcus screamed. Oblivious to the risk, he booted his horse and charged forwards.

As Marcus approached at a breakneck speed, the beast lifted his weapon. All the rider could see was a pair of bright, white specks rising from the pile of white cloth.

Marcus nodded, and clenched his teeth so hard they almost cracked.

The sword swung, sharp blade biting through the cool evening air. Marcus threw himself to the side, yanking the horse around.

Hooves skidded on dry dirt, and Marcus brushed the ground with one hand, skin peeling off on the tiny rocks and sharp stones that dotted the side of the road.

The blade scraped his leg, sending spears of fire shooting through his thigh. Marcus's outstretched hand grabbed Julianne's.

Fingers wrapped around his wrist. He pulled, gripping the

pommel of his saddle with white knuckles. He felt Julianne's leap, pushing her off the ground and her grip on his arm pulled harder.

The horse skidded to a stop, now facing the back of the monstrous, armored creature from another world. Julianne's arms slid around Marcus's waist as the momentum of their turn slid him back to a sitting position.

Now. Julianne's command thundered in his head, and he kicked, bolting forwards. The lumbering man-beast tried to turn, but his heavy armor slowed him. Marcus dashed past, and they were off, hurtling down the road, wind whipping hair into his face and stinging his eyes.

The gates that kept Tahn wrapped in safety had already opened to admit the crowd of people fleeing towards safety. Now, they were closing. Bowmen stood on the wall, tall and proud, weapons drawn.

Two men—one short, the other with sparkling white eyes, screamed from above.

"Faster, Faster!"

"Get yer skinny ass inside ye prick!"

Marcus leaned forwards, kicking his horse and praying it wouldn't stumble.

Something leapt onto the road beside them. Big, red... he didn't look, only focused on the narrowing gap ahead.

Julianne's weight shifted behind him. He felt the scrape of a sword being pulled from his scabbard, then a piercing scream filled the air.

Marcus roared. He kicked harder. The horse slammed through the tiny opening in the gate, slamming Marcus's leg against the barricade, then stumbling to the ground inside the safe confines of Tahn.

Marcus rolled free of the horse's weight, and the animal lurched back to its feet, sweating and trembling.

"Jules?" Marcus gasped.

She crawled over to him, then collapsed, rolling onto her back.

"Bitch be damned," she gasped. "You're insane."

Marcus felt a laugh bubble up. "You're alive because of it."

"I wasn't complaining." She lurched up and leaned her head on his chest. "Thanks for saving my ass."

"Thanks for being ready," he said. "If I'd gotten there, and you hadn't jumped, we'd both be dead."

"It helps that I knew what you were doing," she admitted.

The horse casually clopped over, then lifted its tail.

Marcus and Julianne bolted, rolling away and jumping to their feet.

"I suppose I deserved that," Marcus said, face wrinkling in distaste as the horse proceeded to drop lumps of shit on the road right next to him.

Marcus clapped the horse's rump, then looked up to the watch tower beside the wall. "What's out there?" Marcus called.

"One fat dead bastard, and four fat live bastards," Garrett yelled back down. "And one big prick so ugly he can't show his face."

"Dead?" Marcus called.

He saw Danil nod. "Jules stabbed it with your pointy stick," he said. "Nice work. Wish I had a girl to do all my killing for me."

"Hey!" Polly squealed

Danil winced as she emerged behind him and whacked the back of his head. "It's really not my day, today."

Polly just shook her head and started down the ladder. Danil followed her.

"What are you two doing?" Julianne asked.

"Can't fight from up there," Polly pointed out. "And those bastards look like they want in. How'd you do with the portal?"

Julianne nodded. "All closed up. At least, I think it'll work."

She explained that Ardie had shown her how arduous the trip through the rift was. It seemed the creatures had the same need for air as those on Irth, and that some had died from lack of it.

"So," she finished, "Making sure they get stuck on our end should mean they just suffocate."

Polly winced. "Poor little varks."

Julianne pursed her lips. "I don't think so. We haven't seen a vark come through since the bigger ones. I think the varks were the guinea pigs—they made it through, and now the big guys are traveling through, they don't need to send any more test subjects."

"Where is Ardie?" Marcus asked. "You… you didn't squash him, did you?"

"No, dear." Julianne patted Marcus's hand. "Annie is babysitting. Vark-sitting? Ardie is with her."

"Ah." Marcus tipped his head towards the ladder. "Should we go up for a look?"

Julianne responded by kneeling next to him. "Are you sure you should even be walking on this?" She tenderly touched his blood-soaked thigh.

Marcus shrugged. "It stings, but I think he just grazed it." He bent his knees and shifted his weight. "It's fine."

"Right." Julianne stood and headed for the ladder. "But if you get blood on my robes, you're on washing duty."

She shimmied up the ladder, leaving Marcus to wonder when he *wasn't* on washing duty.

Julianne scanned the flat, open land outside Tahn. The still body of the alien she'd stabbed lay on the road, ignored by its kin. The armored man paced along the wall, occasionally making casual swipes with his blade.

"This shouldn't be too hard," Julianne murmured.

Garrett glanced at her, eyes wide. "Yer havin' me on, right?"

Bette snorted. "Grow some balls, ye wee coward. She's right."

Garrett smiled sweetly. "Ye've got enough balls for three of us, me love."

"Damn right I have," Bette said. "Look. That one there, he might be big, but he's a wee bit stupid. That armor is weighin' him down. Watch him turn…"

Garrett watched as the clobbering thing reached the end of his track, then slowly and awkwardly turned.

"I bet if he had a wee stumble, he'd hit the ground and not get up. He'd be like a wee tortoise, or a big fat roach stuck on its back, legs all AHHH and EEHHH!" Bette scrabbled at the air with her hands, mimicking an upside-down roach.

"Best not piss the bastard off, me love," Garrett pointed out. Her voice had carried through the night air, and the beast in question had slowly turned his head towards her.

It resumed its stomping progress. "The scaly things have hard carapaces," Julianne told them. "But they're not as protected as Ardie."

She lifted her arm and drew a line under her armpit. "There's a gap around here, and one here," she said as her finger traveled down her side. "And they have nothing over their faces. If you can get something sharp in any of those spots, they're dead."

"So, we need to trip the big bastard, then get in close to the others?" Marcus asked.

Julianne pursed her lips. "Maybe not. I think the big one controls the others. If we take him out, his minions might—*might*—leave us alone."

"Well, then," Marcus said. "Let's hope he leads the charge."

CHAPTER TWENTY-EIGHT

Polly stood at the ladder propped on the wall, hands sweaty on her spear. She touched the dagger at her belt gently.

"You've checked that three times now," Danil murmured. "It's definitely there."

She flicked him a nervous grin. "I just want to go already."

"Not until we get the signal." Danil's eyes reflected the moonlight, and Polly wondered if she'd ever seen anything more beautiful.

She eyed the wall before them, leaning on the cottage beside it. Garrett teetered on the top of the ladder, crouched low as he looked over the battlefield outside. A rope dangled from one hand.

"Am I going in blind today?" Danil asked, the white fading from his eyes.

"What?" she yelped. "Don't be stupid. You don't go into a real fight without using every advantage you've got!"

"Fair enough." He shrugged. "I think it'd be great practice, though."

"Don't you dare," she threatened. "Or I'll sneak up behind you and stick this spear up your ass."

He winced. "My cheeks are still smarting from Garrett's bloody—that's it!"

A crash from the gates signaled it was time to go. Garrett flung the rope over the wall and made sure the hooked end was secure. Then, he silently swung a leg over and disappeared.

Danil went next, then it was Polly's turn. She tried to ignore the weakness in her knees as she climbed up and refused to look down as she wrapped her hands around the rope. In moments, her feet were back on solid ground. She tugged the rope to let Mack know he was safe to follow.

"Stay down until we attack," Garrett whispered. He pointed at a lumbering beast not too far off, a little separated from the others. "Our job is to harry the pests, make their ugly-assed owner mad enough to follow us."

The whites of his eyes shined in the moonlight. "Once ye've got his attention, then run. Run! No dickin' about, ye hear? Straight fer the town, and fer the sake of the Queen Bitch herself, do NOT get caught in the trip-wire."

The small party nodded.

"Off we go!" Garrett turned and ran for his target, ducking low in the long grass. Polly quickly lost sight of him.

She made to follow, but Danil caught her arm. "There's another one headed this way." He pointed.

"I don't see it," Polly whispered, eyes straining. She wished the moon was just a little fuller tonight.

"Me neither." Danil's teeth shone in a grin. "But Bette does."

"Oh, you flipping genius," Polly said. With his sight-skills, he would be able to see the whole battlefield, from the perspective of anyone watching.

They scurried off, the whispering grass the only sound to give them away. Danil put an arm out to stop her.

He pointed. Polly lifted her head just far enough to see the hulking creature ambling their way.

"Face, armpits, sides," she muttered to herself. A strike anywhere else would just slide off their hard shells.

GO!

Danil's order bounced into her head, and she shot forwards, spear over her shoulder, ready to stab for the floppy, snouted face of her target.

"*AARGRH!*" Danil's war-cry caught the beast's attention.

It turned, just as Polly thrust forwards. Her spear slammed into the back of its head and snapped in half, jarring her arm. "Shit!"

She pulled back and used the jagged wooden end to ward off the angry glare that turned her way. Sharp, scissor-like claws stabbed forwards, and she danced out of the way.

The attack revealed jagged hooks jutting from the creature's arms. If it got close enough to grab her, she'd be torn apart.

Polly eyed her spear—or, what was left of it. The stick was a little shorter than the beast's reach.

"Let's hope you're not much faster than the old man," she grunted.

Polly slid forwards, then rolled under an angry swipe. She came to her feet behind her opponent. The alien swung around. "Fast," she murmured. "This isn't gonna be easy."

She trained her gaze on the soft spots beneath its arms. If Danil had a chance to slip in there, she wanted to make sure he could see what he was doing.

He took the chance. Polly saw his blade flash, but the beast jerked out of his way.

"Too slow!" she called to Danil.

"I noticed," he called back, sword out as the beast's attention turned to him.

If I can just slip under there, Polly thought, visualizing her next move.

The beast swung back, twisting to protect the vulnerable spot.

That was weird. Polly slowly moved to one side. She blew out a slow breath and pictured herself running forwards, stabbing the flaccid snout with her splintered stick.

The creature whined and spun, turning its back to her.

"Uhh, Danil?" she called. "We might have a small problem."

"This fat bastard is anything *but* small," Danil called. He danced backwards as a claw sliced out towards him. "And it's fast, too."

"So fast it's like it knows your move before you make it?" Polly asked. She darted forwards, then swung back as her target rounded on her.

"Yeah. That fast." Danil stepped back. "Wait a minute. Are you saying…"

"I am. I don't even have to make the move, Danil. Just picture it in my head."

"Well, shit." Danil tried another blow. The beast dodged easily. "My mental shields aren't much use here."

Polly closed her eyes. She felt the wind, heard the rustle of grass. Pictured herself throwing high, towards its face.

Polly ducked as the breeze shifted, opening her eyes. The beast didn't change its strike, claw sailing harmlessly over her head.

"It sees what we visualize!" Polly yelled. "Not what we feel. Danil… you're going in blind, my love."

With a flurry of motion, Danil charged and rolled, coming to his feet behind her, green eyes sparkling.

"Now *this* is gonna be fun." Danil lifted his sword and let his senses absorb his surroundings.

Though Polly had taught him how to fight blind, his sharply honed senses gave him the advantage. Once she had shown him a trick, he could usually use it to best her when she fought blindfolded.

Danil took a slow breath and let it out, feeling his chest sink down. Cool air touched his skin, while the warmth of Polly's skin just inches away soaked into one arm.

He felt a subtle shift in the air. He lunged backwards. Then, he darted forwards. His sword scraped along hard carapace. *Too low*, he thought.

He waited, hearing the rustle of grass as his enemy turned to face him. Again, the shift. This time, Danil angled his blade just a little higher. It clattered against hard shell, then lodged into something soft.

Screams buffered Danil's mind. He thrust harder, twisting the sword in soft flesh. A heavy weight leaned against him, and he drew back, slipping his sword out moments before the beast thumped onto the ground.

A roar echoed in the sky. Danil snapped back into magic mode, using Polly's eyes to see the tall humanoid monster start towards them. It took three steps, then broke into a run—headed right for them.

"Got the bastard," Danil muttered. He kept his mind carefully clear of predictions—the last thing he wanted was to tip the asshole off about the trap they'd laid.

He turned and ran, angling back towards the gates of Tahn.

The ground shook with each clomping stride the giant took. Armor clanked, and, in the distance, Danil heard cries of warning.

"Pull yer panties up, boys! It's comin'!" Bette yelled.

Ahead, the small group of fighters Danil had scaled the wall with were headed inside. Behind, the thundering crashes were getting closer. Danil glanced to the side. Polly ran beside him, grinning.

"You're—you're not even... tired?" he gasped, pumping his legs as hard as they could go.

"Tired? Ha!" Polly leapt ahead, legs like a gazelle. She turned back to check on him, and her eyes widened in alarm. "Move it, kid! It's right on your tail!"

Kid? Danil thought. *More like a tired old man. What the fuck am I doing out here?*

Julianne stood atop the wall, watching his flight across the open field. Through her eyes, he saw the small figure running and stumbling, chased by the larger, heavier beast. Neither were particularly fast, or graceful.

Pride prickled him. He didn't like Julianne seeing his desperate progress. Remembering how Polly had shown him how to run more gracefully, Danil lengthened his stride, straightened his back and timed his breath to his steps.

He saw the difference. Less stooped, he made a bigger target, but his speed increased just enough. He saw the fat rope strung across the path and jumped, pulling his legs up and praying he didn't end up as the fly caught in the web.

He made it, stumbled, then righted himself. Inside the gates, he stopped to watch.

The lumbering Skrima followed but slowed, pulling up before the rope. It leaned forwards, bunched its legs, then jumped over the rope.

The whole village fell silent for a breath. Then, the monster took its next running step.

A second tripwire, this one a thick steel wire, caught its boot. The beast lurched forwards, toppling onto the ground with a mighty crash.

Bette's victorious holler was quickly joined by others. Bodies rushed the flailing Skrima, climbing on it, stabbing metal and wood against the hard shell of its armor.

Danil leaned forwards to rest his hands on his knees. He saw Polly, rushing to stab at a knee joint. Her first strike slid off, but a second plunged deep, splattering crimson ichor as she withdrew the stumpy spear.

She'd stopped to pick it up, Danil realized, still dazed and oxygen starved from his frantic run.

He almost didn't notice someone move up to stand next to him.

"You look like shit." Julianne rested a hand on his back, and

Danil's mind flooded with gentle energy, while the tightness in his chest eased.

He knew it was a false sensation but enjoyed it anyway.

"Thanks. I love being told how handsome I am." He nodded at the fallen Skrima. "Looks like this little adventure is done."

"We've won the battle." Julianne's smile held a hint of sadness. "Not the war."

"You think there's more than one portal, don't you?" Danil asked.

"Do you really believe there's not?" Julianne asked.

He shook his head. "Not really. I'd like to pretend, though. Just for tonight?"

Julianne really smiled then, a grin that lit up her eyes. "I think we can do that."

CHAPTER TWENTY-NINE

Tansy strummed the strings of the little banjo in time to Garrett's raucous words.

And so, did I say
On that fateful day
To the man with the little tiny dick
I said if ye dare
Then I'll grab ye by the hair
Of yer balls and I'll kill ye right quick
He ducked, and he rolled
And he was so bold
He still tried to sneak off to me lass
But I knew he were there
So, I grabbed his curly hair
And shoved my wee sword up his ass

Bette hooted and slapped her knee, while Tansy let out a melodious yodel.

Julianne nudged Danil and pointed. Amongst the press of bodies twisting and twirling on the floor in time to the rearick ballad, Annie and Cavill danced.

Annie had her skirts lifted almost to her knees while her

quick feet stepped in time to the music. Cavill's hands twisted in the air as he kept time with her, both of them red-faced in the warmth and grinning like children.

"That's adorable!" Julianne exclaimed, grinning as widely as Annie herself.

"It's pretty sweet," Danil said. He'd only stepped off the floor a short time earlier, after Polly finally took pity on his aching feet. "Annie's outdoing half the damn town, though. She hasn't stopped!"

"To be fair, she didn't have to sprint across a giant field with a big, mean monster on her heels," Julianne teased.

Danil laughed. "That big, mean monster almost had my ass!"

"Polly would have gone back for you." Julianne looked up as Marcus wandered over to hand her a brass cup.

She sipped it, closing her eyes. "Mary broke out the good stuff tonight," she mused, swaying in time to the next song. This time, Tessa crooned a slow song about a young girl who was leaving her home for the first time, off on an adventure to a faraway city.

Marcus took Julianne's hand and pulled her away from Danil. "Dance with me," he begged.

Julianne shot Danil an apologetic look, but he waved her off.

"See! Julianne's dancing!" a voice said in his ear.

"Polly, I can barely stand!" Danil complained. Still, he grinned when she passed him a plate loaded with roast beef, gravy, potatoes, and bread.

"This should perk you up," she said.

"Or send me into a food coma," Danil said through a mouthful of food.

"Oh, for Bitch's sake, at least sit down." Polly dabbed a napkin on his shirt where he'd already dripped some gravy.

"Yes, boss." Danil shuffled over to a seat and balanced the plate on his lap. He sighed happily.

"I knew a good feed would cheer you up," Polly said.

"A plate like this could cheer up a dead remnant," Danil

pointed out. "Have you tasted this beef? I've seen melted butter that's tougher."

Polly picked a morsel off his plate and put it in her mouth. She closed her eyes in bliss.

Danil leaned over and kissed her cheek. Polly's eyes snapped open in surprise. "What was that for?" she asked.

"Because I love you." He held out another bit of meat and popped it in her mouth.

"Oh. Well, I am quite lovable." She opened her mouth, waiting for another bite.

Danil put the plate down. "Food can wait," he said, standing. "Tonight, we dance."

He swept her out into the crowded dance floor and twirled her around. "Tonight, we dance. Tomorrow, we fight. Then, we eat."

"Sounds like a perfect date." Polly twirled around, then drew in close to him and rested her head on his chest.

"Just perfect," he said, resting a hand on her head.

FINIS

Wow, guys, long time no see!

I feel like I owe you all a bit of an apology, or at least an explanation. Christmas/New Year's was an utterly CRAZY time for me. We moved to our beautiful new dream house in a tiny valley town. We had no internet for about three weeks (hullo, astronomical phone bill!) and my kids were on the equivalent of what I think is the US summer break - seven weeks of summer break, trapped inside due to constant rain and an unfinished yard, overly-excited about the new changes but also incredibly anxious about new schools.

It was incredible, but also hell. Writing didn't come close to being on schedule, but I'm trying to be ok with that - after all, family comes first! Still, not having my writing, which is kind of a sanity break amongst the chaos, might have made me a bit of a cranky beast.

This year, I expect things to be a little smoother. My smallest has started day care, and apart from tantrums on the days she goes (because she doesn't want to leave) and the days she doesn't (because she wants to be there), it's going really well!

Side note: I just leaned over to type a note to Steve and Jami, that

"I'm just knocking up my author notes now". Steve was a little perturbed until I explained I like my notes to gestate for a while, then emerge fresh and pink and wailing, and make everyone in the room cry tears of joy. Please, feel free to cry while reading this.

Anyway... Broken Bones, the next part of the vagina-rift arc, is underway and shouldn't be too long of a wait. I've got two weeks of school holidays in the middle, because the school system exists purely to torture parents, but daycare will continue so I'm hoping my middle kid is old enough to respond to hard cash bribery so I can keep working.

Ok, now Steve is going to be a character in one of Jami's books. I can't wait to read that one...

I hope you guys have a really happy Easter, which falls a few days after you'll get this book. If you see me online begging for wine a few days after that, it's because the bribery didn't work. Send babysitters.

Happy reading!

Amy

AUTHOR NOTES - MICHAEL ANDERLE
MARCH 26, 2018

First, THANK YOU for not only reading this story, but our author notes here in the very, very, very back as well.

Now, I KNOW I'm not supposed to laugh at other's trials in life, but Amy makes it so damned hard NOT to. If I go to hell for laughing at your shit, Hopkins, I'm totally grabbing you on the way down.

Just saying.

It is pretty damned amazing what our little group of friends (family if you will) have gone off to do since we started all of these collaborations a little over a year ago. Houses have been bought (I don't know if LMBPN books had anything to do w/ Amy's new house, but I do know of two other authors who have purchased homes due to their success) and careers have been supported and helped.

Not every effort went well, unfortunately, and I hold out hope that some of the series will catch on as we re-cover the books and figure out how to get them back into the market for another swing.

For example: this series is going under the knife and we are going to redo the covers.

This is a TYPICAL type of interaction with Amy when stuff goes down. I'm beginning to wonder if it is a typical AUSSIE type response and if it is? *Then I need more Aussie's in my life, you people are fucking hilarious!*

Imagine this: Jude delivers the following image to us in SLACK (our company communication platform). Jude is just trying to get an idea if we are moving in the right direction because 3D can be very challenging and sucks to have to undo a lot of work or start over.

When I see the image, my answer is a very simple: "Oooohhh. I like this!"

Amy's however, is this: "I love it and hubby thinks she's hot and wants to meet her, so.... good?"

I'm just wondering what kind of relationship she has with hubby? Because, my Hispanic wife wouldn't react the same way.

At all.

Period.

I think Amy's books deserve a fresh effort and a lot of time has been spent thinking HOW to do it. Covers are usually the first to be considered (after story.)

THANK YOU SO MUCH for reading (and reviewing, and telling friends) about our work. It is because of you that WE get to write for a living!

Ad Aeternitatem,

Michael Anderle

CONNECT WITH THE AUTHORS

Amy Hopkins Social
Website:
https://amyhopkinsauthor.com
Facebook:
https://www.facebook.com/thespellscribe

Connect with Michael Anderle

Website: http://lmbpn.com
Email List: http://lmbpn.com/email/

Social Media:

https://www.facebook.com/LMBPNPublishing
https://twitter.com/lmbpn
https://www.instagram.com/lmbpn_publishing/
https://www.bookbub.com/authors/michael-anderle

Realm of the Nine Circles

www.ingramcontent.com/pod-product-compliance
Lightning Source LLC
Chambersburg PA
CBHW05025711 0726
47898CB00007B/2448